Where the Long Grass Bends

where
the
long
grass
bends

STORIES

Neela
Vaswani

Neela Vaswani

Sarabande Books

LOUISVILLE, KENTUCKY

Managing Editor
Sarabande Books, Inc.
2234 Dundee Road, Suite 200
Louisville, KY 40205

LIBRARY OF CONGRESS CATALOGING-IN-PUBLICATION DATA

Vaswani, Neela, 1974–
    Where the long grass bends : stories / by Neela Vaswani.—1st ed.
        p.   cm.
    ISBN 1-889330-96-5 (pbk. : alk. paper)
1. India—Social life and customs—Fiction. 2. East Indian Americans—
Fiction. I. Title.
PS3622.A86 W48 2004
813'.6—dc21   2003003869

Cover image by Greg McHale

Manufactured in the United States of America
This book is printed on acid-free paper.

Sarabande Books is a nonprofit literary organization.

This project is supported in part by an award from the National
Endowment for the Arts.

NATIONAL
ENDOWMENT
FOR THE ARTS   FIRST EDITION

For my parents

Table of Contents

Where the Long Grass Bends

Where
the Long
Grass Bends

What difference does my conception make? I am here. How that came to be is not important.

Yesterday, two of the Sisters walked me between them to the edge of the cliff and told me I was not born of rape. I think this must be what they tell every child like me; something false crusted their speech, something practiced and charitable. Underneath the pipal tree, where the bats hang upside-down, the Sisters told me I was born of love, a love polar and incongruous. My mother was Gharwali and my father British. They orphaned me in the lake where they drowned, drowned each other. In trying to keep their own selves afloat, they pushed the other down, again and again, under the water. I never knew them.

Where the Long Grass Bends

At the mission, I am the only child with yellow hair and a black face. I hear there is another like me, a boy, who lives at the bottom of the cliff with the sadhus. Among the children it is said that the boy's father is the man who shakes the pipal tree at midday. The man smiles as the bats smash into his body and the trees and the walls of the mission church. Chris the Colonist, he calls himself; so we do, too.

Not all the children who go to school here are orphans. At the end of the day, most walk down the mountain to their homes, to their mothers and fathers. I watch them go, staying under the pipal tree, looking down to where the long grass bends. Today, as I stand with the slitted eyes of the bats all around me, I do not like the name Elizabeth. No one I know gave it to me—a name as cold and dark as deep water.

Because their parents told them so, the children believed the tension of elections started the riots. The Sisters and I knew that without the sixth-grade exams there would have been no trouble.

The day of the test, the Sisters called in the police and asked them to surround the school. In past years, parents had stood outside the windows of the mission and shouted answers to their children, or tried to bribe the test proctors

4

with money and home-cooked sweets. This year was no exception, and around the ring of police, a semicircle of parents formed, shouting and shoving: "Meechu! Meechu! Don't forget the square root of 81 is 9 and the prefix *neo* means new!" I stood under the pipal tree. When I take the exam in two years, no one will shout to me and I am glad for that.

I looked down the cliff and saw a large group of people parading on the mission road. They held election signs and sang. They advanced up the mountain to the school, and then the election group shoved and shouted at the parents who in turn shoved and shouted at the police, and so began the riots. I stayed under the pipal tree with the bats. One person died, an old man trampled by the crowd. No one seemed to know who he was or where he came from, and two weeks into the war, no one remembered the role the sixth-grade exams had played in the violence.

It was during this war—a little war, but a war all the same—that I learned how small a space I could fit myself into.

In the third week of riots, the local government demanded that classes end. The rebels in favor of the Dalit candidate were believed to be hiding in the thick forest around the mission. The government issued shoot-on-sight orders for the one road leading from the mission to town, and police patrolled the area. They traveled by foot or scooter. One drove up and down the mountain in a car. He had stars on his uniform and carried a *lathi* cut from a neem tree. It smelled of garlic.

The Sisters continued school on the rise above the garbage pit. Since the town children were unable to get up the road, only boarder students attended class. At first, the Sisters taught us all together, regardless of age and ability, but an edict declaring groups of more than three people to be seditious and revolutionary forced them to stop. Then the Sisters took two students at a time to the rise above the garbage pit and taught the day's lesson. If we heard anyone approaching, we tossed our books into the dump and lay back comfortably, as if resting in the sun. Whoever said his times-tables slowest was made to clamber down the stinking, slick sides of the dump to retrieve the books. I never had to.

This arrangement lasted about a week before the government sent a policeman with a machine gun and bullet belt to patrol the garbage pit. We began meeting in the chapel. Because we lived at the mission, the police assumed us to be Christian. They let us alone when we studied inside the church. Kneeling on the pews as the Sisters taught class, we were prepared to tuck our lesson-books behind the Bibles and assume an attitude of prayer.

Where the Long Grass Bends

. . .

On election day, another student and I sat in the chapel learning geography. We smelled torch-smoke and heard chanting, angry choruses and refrains; we pushed our books into the pew-backs. The Sister and the other child ran from the church. I do not know why I stayed behind.

I heard the mob-chants fragment into disorderly yelling; I heard the Sister's voice praying for mercy, mercy for her and the child. Her scale of Hail Marys climbed in pitch and the child screamed and screamed and then they both were silent. I still cannot remember the child's name.

I looked for a place to hide. The church was open and bare except for a grand piano that had been donated by a British widow in the year of Independence. Only one Sister could play the piano, but she was frail and often sick. When she felt well, she pounded out hymns. I hummed along. The music was nice but I did not like the words.

Dropping to my hands and knees, I crawled to the piano. Dust moved in the roads of light filtering through the cross-shaped windows. I climbed the piano bench, then stood on the covered keyboard. Using all of my strength to hoist up the top of the piano, I balanced the edge of the lid on my shoulders and propped it open with the thin, lacquered stick. The stick looked too small to support the lid—shaped like a subcontinent, heavy as a

7

subcontinent. Sideways, I slipped inside the piano and kicked the stick until it folded. The lid slammed down, and I heard the mob enter the chapel.

For once, I was glad to be small.

In the guts of the piano with my knees drawn to my chin, I lay on my side. Wires pressed meanly into my arms; wooden hammers knuckled my back. I heard the mob faintly now, as the walls of the piano muffled sound. When smoke seeped inside, I coughed into my hair.

I do not know and will never know how many people moved the piano. It suddenly jerked forward, and the back of my head slammed into the felt-tipped hammers. The piano moved perversely, first in one direction, then another, as if those who pushed it were not in agreement. I knew when we exited the church because of the cool, smokeless air passing through the strip of space between the lid and body of the instrument. Still, the mob shoved at the piano and, wedged inside, I lurched along, too. When I heard the shrieks of disrupted bats, I knew we were rolling under the pipal tree, toward the edge of the cliff. Then the piano stopped moving. I kissed my knees and snapped piano wires with my feet. The mob-sounds drifted away.

My crunched bones ached. I listened to the inner ticks and sprangs of the piano till I was sure of the silence, and then I decided to lift the lid, to unfold myself and see what shape I was in. I wiggled till I kneeled on the bent wires and row of hammers, then squared my shoulders and heaved. The lid lifted easily.

The piano was perched on the edge of the cliff, under the pipal tree and the regrouped, slumbering bats. Below spanned the road, a capital "S" slithering down the mountain. At the first curve of the road, I saw the mob circling a burning police car.

A flaming man rolled from the car and onto the street. The mob surged forward and put his fire out with rocks and fists, then reset the fire and chanted faster and faster. He took a long time to burn into a small pile, and the mob waited patiently till he disappeared. I smelled his flesh; it smelled like my own, smoky and sour. The mob had uncovered the keyboard so when I stepped from the piano, my feet pronounced a quick din of incompatible chords.

Walking under the pipal tree, I slammed into the chest of Chris the Colonist: he hung upside-down, his legs hooked over a low branch. He was barechested in a white dhoti. His long yellow hair pointed at the ground, and his face and neck looked purple.

"Hello, Jarasandha," he said. "One day you should come and see my leeches."

"That's not my name," I replied, and like the bats, he closed his eyes into slits.

Where the Long Grass Bends

I stood looking at him, at his yellow hair, till the Sisters found me and put me to bed. They told me that my teacher and the child whose name I cannot remember had been killed. The mob left their fractured bodies inside the chapel. One Sister gave me a hot-water bottle. She said it would comfort me. Last year, when I had pneumonia, they gave me a rosary. I broke it in half to make a set of beaded anklets.

In the house where I slept, there was a toilet with no flush. Two buckets of water triggered the siphon and swirled everything away. When the Sisters left, I added the water from my hot-water bottle to the flushing bucket, then lay in bed listening to the rats scout the hall. Outside, the mists hung mute and private. I opened the window, curious to see if the fog would enter my room in a mass; instead, a man with a bloody cut on his forehead appeared and dropped onto my bed. I think he was afraid he had landed on my legs. He patted the bed all around till he touched my feet, then nodded contentedly at the wall. I liked him then. He sat on the bed, and I took my pillowcase from my pillow, stood on tiptoe, and wrapped it around his head. I put my finger to my lips to silence him. When he crawled under my bed, I handed him the deflated hot- water bottle.

"To comfort you," I said.

Every night for two weeks, he appeared in the same

way and slept in the same place. I washed my pillowcase in the flushing bucket and poured the stained water down the toilet so the Sisters would not find his blood and look for him. Later, I saw his face in the newspaper and read that he was the rebel leader. He knew I could keep a secret. This is the first time I have told.

The Sisters found him in the chapel and turned him in. After his capture, the little war petered out and school resumed its normal schedule. The sixth graders were not allowed to retake their exam although they and their parents claimed the noise of the old man's death had lowered the scores. Weekends, the Sisters volunteered at the hospital and brought me with them. They left me on a gurney while they talked to patients. I played dice with the lepers. I let them touch my yellow hair, and they let me touch their cratered sores. One afternoon, the nurses projected *The Longest Day* onto the wall of the waiting room, and I fell asleep watching it. What is a fake war when you have seen a real one? And with the shoot-on-sight orders rescinded, I began sneaking down the mountain, crouching in the long grass after dark. I wanted to see the boy, the boy with yellow hair and a black face, like me. I wanted to see the leeches of Chris the Colonist.

• • •

Chris the Colonist found me as I hunted him. Through the long grass, he slithered behind me and held my ankles firmly when I tried to escape.

"Why are you here, Jarasandha?" he asked.

Into the dark night and shushing grass I said, "That is not my name."

He carried me under his arm to his hut built over the marshes. "The best leeches live there," he said, pointing to the farthest stretch of wet, sunken land.

To get to his hut, we crossed a bridge of stones poking through the black sludge. Inside, glass terrariums covered the dirt floor, all of them filled with leeches. Chris the Colonist dropped me onto his mattress and walked to the cages.

"Hello, sweeties, I brought someone for you to meet," he whispered into the screened tops. I was not afraid of him. He is crazy, but he bounces on the balls of his feet when he walks and no one who does that can be bad.

He told me he would feed his most prized leeches at midnight; he showed me the ones he had bred to be green with a line of orange spots. There were giant leeches, too, the length of one strand of my hair, the width of the Colonist's arm.

"Genetics," he said, as he lifted out a striped leech, "is a beautiful thing, to be manipulated and mixed, to make something new." Near the window I saw a pile of dead bats.

He attached seven leeches to his calves, stomach, and arms. I helped him adhere seven more to his back. Then I offered up my own arms and legs, and we lay together on his mattress, nourishing the leeches and making them fat. I felt a little dizzy. After three minutes, the Colonist expertly plucked the leeches from my limbs and replaced them with new ones. Small points of blood spotted my legs and arms. While I was there, he did not feed the giant leeches.

The next night, I hid in the long grass and waited till I felt the Colonist's hands around my ankles. Again, he carried me under his arm to his hut. He knew I would not run away if he set me down, but he said he was used to carrying the bats this way and I let him do the same with me.

When I asked him why he called me Jarasandha he said he would not answer until I asked the correct question. He avoided attaching leeches to the tiny scabs on my legs and arms where they had fed the night before. After using me for one feeding, he took two giant leeches and plastered them to his own back. "Who is Jarasandha?" I asked, and leaning over his legs with the leeches stuck to his back, the Colonist told me. I had asked the right question.

. . .

Long, long ago, before the British, before the Mughals, King Brihadratha ruled Magadha. He had two wives, twin sisters, neither of whom had borne him a son.

When a powerful sage came to Magadha, the king lavished him with presents. The offerings pleased the sage, who had recently renewed his strength by standing in fire for seven years. He granted the king a boon.

"Oh, great one," sighed the king, "what need have I for a boon? I am about to renounce my kingdom and go into the forest for I have no son."

The rishi closed his eyes and focused on the king's problem. So strong was the wind of his thought that a woman walking past was lifted and blown to the top of Mount Kailash. After some time, a mango dropped from the heavens into the sage's lap. Handing the fruit to the king, he said, "Have your wife eat this, and you will be given a son."

Brihadratha felt he could not give the mango to only one queen. So, as he walked, the king split the mango. He gave half to one sister and half to the other. Nine months later, each queen delivered half a baby. Their midwives carried the two lifeless pieces into the forest, behind the royal apartments, and left them near some ferns.

Just then, Jara, the man-eating rakshasi, walked by. The smell of human flesh led her to the dead pieces. So they would be easier to carry back to her lair, she joined them. The moment she connected the two halves, the baby came to life and cried in her arms. Hearing the cries, the king, the queens, and the midwives came running. Jara handed the baby to the virtuous king saying, "I, Jara, have saved your baby. Take him, he is yours."

"Good rakshasi," replied the king, "as it was you who put him together and made him whole, he shall be named Jarasandha."

As the years passed, Jarasandha grew into a conceited and ambitious king. Lord Krishna and his cousins, the Pandava brothers, learned of Jarasandha's tyranny and decided to fight and kill him. They traveled to King Jarasandha's court and asked him for a single combat.

At the city arena, Jarasandha and Bhima, the mightiest Pandava, fought till their maces broke. For twenty-seven days they continued to fight, but were so evenly matched that neither man ever wounded or beat the other. On the twenty-eighth day, as Bhima was about to enter the arena, he appealed to Lord Krishna, "Please, tell me how to defeat Jarasandha."

Krishna picked up a twig and split it down the middle into two separate pieces. Bhima understood.

During the wrestling match, Bhima seized the king's legs and threw him to the ground. Standing on one of

Jarasandha's feet, he grabbed hold of the other and tore the body of the king in two, flinging the halves far away from each other. Thus ended Jarasandha's life.

I looked at the Colonist. His face was colored a sickly white, and he fainted as I asked him, "Are you all right?" I pried the two giant leeches from his back and put them in their cages. Then I draped some blankets around him and left the hut, thinking of my yellow hair and black face.

This morning, Saturday, I told the Sisters I felt tired so I would not have to go to the hospital and sit with the lepers. I wanted to explore the woods around the mission.

I took the path that climbed up the mountain, away from the long grass and the Colonist's hut. As I walked, light and shadow stuttered through the tree trunks. I remembered what the rebel leader had told me about the grass. He said, "When you see the long grass and fear its height and the terror that might hide in its thickness, just think, yes, the grass is long, but because it is long, it will bend, and I will see what it hides."

Picking at the leech-scabs on my arms, I climbed the mountain into the dank, chilly clouds. I had not been above the mission for many months.

Where the Long Grass Bends

When I reached the summit, I saw a claw-foot bathtub on a shelf of mica. The wind blew roughly; I felt cold. A boy with yellow hair and a black face suddenly popped his head over the side of the tub and roared like a panther. "Look at the fangs on me," he said. I remembered that the tub had belonged to the British widow. She donated it to the Sisters along with the piano. The Sisters, ever charitable, donated the tub to the sadhus because of their matted hair. There was gold plating on the clawed feet.

Springing from the tub, the boy came toward me. I noticed that he walked on the balls of his feet, and I was glad to find him, glad to see him. Small scabs covered his legs and arms.

"What's your name?" I asked, pleased to see him staring at my yellow hair.

"Jarasandha," he said.

"Did you feed the Colonist's leeches?" I extended my scabbed arms.

"Who? These are from the marsh. The sadhus tell me not to wade there but I like it. This is our tub."

"I know someone who grows leeches. He walks on the balls of his feet, too."

"Who cares? Do you want to sit in my tub?"

I did want to sit in the tub. We jumped inside and lay back against the cold porcelain. We unplugged the stopper and pushed our fingers through the broken drain to the ground.

"Do you have a father?" I asked him.

"Do you?" he answered.

"He drowned," I said. "That's what the Sisters tell me."

"Mine is crazy. The sadhus won me from him in a gambling bet."

"Oh." I did not tell him about the Colonist.

So I would have more room, he curled his feet under his thighs. I liked him then. I leaned my head against his thin chest, and he patted my yellow head. We lay flat and comfortable against the curved sides of the tub, watching the light and shadow skip across the sky.

Oh, the comfort of finding a boy with yellow hair and a black face!

Oh, the comfort of sitting with him in a tub, the sadhus and the Sisters and the Colonist far below us, far below, where the long grass bends.

For Kapil and Tara

Possession
at the
Tomb of
Sayyed
Pir Hazrat
Baba Bahadur
Saheed
Rah Aleh

The Spirits, Anger and Sorrow

My name is Gussa, and last Thursday I came to live inside this woman. As she rolled out her prayer rug I was shaken loose from the crook in the Tree of Life where I had lazed for forty-three years. Out of the carpet weft, past the easterly *mihrab* and shabby fringe, I sailed into the woman's intestines. For a week I waited, wandering by her bladder, squeezing around her sockets. I missed the dry rug, the opinions of the wool, sometimes irritating and judgmental like the sheep it had grown from, but still, a familiar voice. It is never easy to leave a place of comfort. The dangerous pumping of this woman's heart and the emissions of her liver frightened me. I hid at the base of her skull, an area of some peace. Then the woman and her daughters were invited to a wedding where she ate seven and a half *ladoos*. In her veins, I saw the linear structure of glucose sweep by. It excited me. Lengthening, I soused the woman's lungs. She ran to the tomb. It was Thursday. Up her throat I spiraled, branching off and down and plunging into her arms. She pounded on the floor, she hollered and grunted, and I, I minced along her tongue. Reaching her teeth, I pushed through the stained gaps. And all of this I did, all of it, so she could roar, "Why did you not ask *me* how *I* felt?"

My name is Dukkha, and twenty Thursdays ago, I came to live inside this child. From the smoke of her mother's funeral pyre I detached myself and flew up her nose. Warm and moist, I stayed hidden in the short cilia, gripping tightly when she sneezed. For weeks I swung there, small but persistent. When she slept, I elongated and spread myself into the bumpy folds of her cerebellum, the canals of her tiny ears. I was sneaky and silent. And one afternoon, the child stepped down from the stool that she used to reach the stovetop. She left the lentils to burn in the pot. She left her brother's math equations blank, and her father's shirt, twice her length from skull to toe, she put aside with an unmended tear. The tires of her uncle's bicycle she left flat, and she ignored her grandfather's gritty feet. As she walked to the temple to garland Ganesha, to pat his trunk and say hello, I sloshed back and forth in her ears. It was the scent of marigolds that finally released me. As the girl extended her hand to the Lord's nose, I shot into her legs, down past her pointed knees and wormed into her toes, as small as peas. She ran to the tomb. It was Thursday. On the ground she curled up, puny and tight; she rocked back and forth. I slid into the corners of her eyes, careful to avoid the gravel there, and then she cried, she moaned and grieved, and sometimes she shouted in her squeaky voice, "I miss my mother, I miss her. Let me have a life of my own."

The Tomb

Climb up a long flight of white marble stairs and you will come to a white marble doorway. Through this doorway you enter a room with a white marble ceiling and four white marble walls. In the center of the room stands a white marble rectangle: nine feet high, three feet wide, and six feet long. Inside the tomb lies Sayyed Pir Hazrat Baba Bahadur Saheed Rah Aleh, a heap of rotting white bones and white cloth. Behind the tomb is another marble doorway. Go through it and you will find yourself in an open-air courtyard with brown brick walls. If you go on a

Where the Long Grass Bends

Monday, Tuesday, Wednesday, Friday, Saturday, or Sunday, you will see only young Farouk, sweeping the dirt floor, resting for a smoke, scouring the walls with a wire brush, looking up into the sky, sprinkling bleach and rose water, scratching the back of his leg with a bare foot.

But if you go on a Thursday, Farouk won't be there, and you will be forced to remain in the doorway. There will be no space for you to sit, to walk about. You will stand there and see fifty-odd women (rarely does the pure spirit bewitch a man) all possessed, but only on Thursdays. They are crammed close against each other, howling, thrashing, sweating, and ranting. And you will see the men who accompany the women. These men squeeze their eyes shut against spit, they dodge kicks and swipes, teeth and knuckles, curses and threats. It takes Farouk six whole days of hard work, some praying, and a bit of loafing, to make the courtyard clean again.

This Thursday, there is one man with two sets of raised pink scratches running in parallel lines down his cheeks. His name is Gopal, and he is here with his possessed wife, Apsara, and their son, their only child, Nanak.

Apsara, Gopal, and Nanak

"THE SPIRIT WANTS TO DRINK A SALTY *LASSI*." Apsara bellows to Gopal, who sits on her stomach. He inclines his head toward their child, but does not loosen his grip around Apsara's wrists.

"Quick quick, fetch one fetch one," she croons to Nanak. Her eyes, her own eyes, blink at him before scrolling up, white again. The boy hesitates. Unless his mother looks at him once more, he will refuse to go. Focusing on Apsara's forehead, webbed with black hair, Nanak thinks, *See me, see me*. Slowly, her eyes roll down, the pupils shrink, then dilate. She sees him. From the ground near his father's foot, the boy snatches coins and runs away.

It is noon, and already the spirit has demanded 7500 rupees worth of goods, mostly kitchenware—a food processor with interchangeable blades, a no-stick frying pan, a glass teapot that the spirit specified whistle, but not too shrilly, and a diamond-chip nose ring. These items were purchased and presented to Apsara. Promises, such as "I'll buy the teapot tomorrow after work," angered the spirit, causing Apsara to hiss and jerk. Excuses, such as "Please, Spirit, we do not have a lot of money. Why don't you go inhabit our neighbor, Jajit, who has a satellite television," forced the spirit into Apsara's long hands. Her fingers curved, then clawed, seeking skin. Sometimes a patter of compliments, praising the spirit's strength and ability to frighten, formed a perceptible ripple that traveled up the length of Apsara's body. After these episodes, the woman smiled and seemed to sleep for a few minutes.

When the nose ring was thrust in front of Apsara's blank eyes, the spirit left the woman abruptly. Apsara coughed and spat blood. She sat up, ruffled Nanak's hair, and touched her husband's scratched cheeks. She pulled a dull gold stud from her nose, twirled in the new starry diamond, and looped her hair into a tidy knot. Then the spirit returned, slamming Apsara onto her back with such force that both of her feet flew up, one after the other, and whacked Gopal in the groin.

Auntie Is Useful

Three years in a row Nanak has seen his mother possessed by the same spirit. It always arrives at dawn on Independence Day—August 15th—when his father's favorite liquor store is closed, and a sign, DRY DAY, hangs crooked on the door. If Independence Day does not fall on a Thursday, the spirit lurks inside Apsara until midnight of the following Wednesday, at which time it detonates, caterwauls, and they all race to the tomb. Gopal holds his wife as the spirit bucks and twists through her. He begs Nanak to buy him a bottle of whiskey, to bring it to him with a Coca-Cola. Then the spirit enters Apsara's mouth. Her sweat-shined lips curl and she snarls, "Irresponsible Drunk, Wastrel, Poor Provider, One-Testicled Sot," until Gopal whimpers, "No more whiskey, I swear it. Release me, release my wife. Forgive." The spirit possessing Apsara is more aggressive and greedy than those controlling the women who convulse and wail around her on the floor. The other husbands nod respectfully to Gopal. He does not notice them.

Friday, the spirit disappears from Apsara, leaving behind a cloud of pale yellow smoke. The family runs from the tomb of Sayyed Pir Hazrat Baba Bahadur Saheed Rah Aleh and goes home to sleep. And on that day Nanak's 250-pound auntie arrives, in a bicycle rickshaw, with her fifty-pound padlocked trunks. Nanak longs to see the insides of these trunks, longs to crouch in one, listening to his aunt's voice fray with worry as she calls his name, searching for him. She tells the boy stories about the wicked suitors she has rescued her daughter from. "Nanak, sweetie, you would not believe," she says, coyly drawing a fuchsia *chunni* across her face, "These men will grow mustaches and beards to hide their cruel lips, but a good Brahmin girl, like myself, always finds them out. You are lucky to have nice plump lips. Be proud; stick them out." Puffing air between his teeth and closed lips, Nanak forms his breath into a ball, then juggles it back and forth in his cheeks. The swishing sounds loud inside his own head, but Auntie does not hear it. "Soon, you will be a young man, Nanak. In four, five years. I suggest you do not grow a mustache." She swings the boy onto her broad lap.

Auntie smells of *hing*, sulfuric and rotten. During the week that she cares for Nanak, she wears the same *salwar kameez*, but changes her *chunni* and spacious underwear daily. She will not allow Nanak to see his parents. They hear his father crying and pacing upstairs; they hear his mother making fresh lime sodas in the kitchen. She carries the drinks on a copper tray, ice cubes clinking, seltzer fizzing quietly. Sometimes she calls out, "Having fun, you two?" and waits until they chorus, "Yes," before mounting the stairs.

Together, the boy and his aunt sit on the tiled parlor floor rolling red marbles up alleys of grout. Auntie tells Nanak, "Maybe your father will end his sickness this time. Maybe, maybe. Some things are very difficult. You understand, don't you, baby?"

Nanak, The Shoe-Finder

With the coins pressed inside his left fist, Nanak darts out of the tomb. At the head of the marble stairs he checks for the spirit's food processor, frying pan, and teapot. He finds them, half-buried beneath a spreading hill of shoes: black rubber, red leather; brown cloth, pink plastic. Since he and his parents were among the first people at the possession, the boy pockets the coins and throws himself, face-down, onto the pile of shoes. He rams his arms deep into the jumble, his right and left hands searching away from each other. Empty heels and toes kick into his stomach. The mixed smell of foreign feet is confusing, so Nanak closes his eyes and rests his cheek on a slipper.

He envisions the green of his own shoes, he smells the crumbled-dirt scent of his feet and closes his hands tightly around two canvas toes. When the boy pulls his arms free of the pile, he sees that he has guessed correctly. In each hand, he holds one of his own green canvas shoes. He claps them, sole to sole, above his head and announces to the sky, "I am Nanak, The Shoe-Finder!"

At the center of the courtyard, a fountain gargles. He skips to it over green and blue tiles and slips into his shoes. Wind gusts through the fall of water, lightly spraying the boy. Laughing, he jumps up and down, his feet smacking into his rump, the ground, his rump, the ground. He listens to the water bubble, the shrieks of possessed women. He cannot distinguish his mother's voice from the others. Holding one knee to his chest, he hops out of the courtyard chanting, *lassi lassi lassi*, as he goes.

How to Make a Salty Lassi

Fill a glass, almost to the top, with plain yogurt, preferably homemade. If you must use store-bought yogurt, keep it at the back of the refrigerator and age it about two months. Only the seasoned nose will be able to discern if the yogurt has soured beyond edibility. It should smell rather strong. Do not worry about the greenish liquid skimming the surface of the yogurt. This is normal, and to be expected. Now, fill the rest of the glass with ice cubes, or water, depending on how much effort you want to put into making the *lassi*, and if you have an electric blender or not. If you are tired and do not have an electric blender, you must use water to fill the remainder of the glass. Use ice cubes and blend if you have a blender; if you have only spoons, use water and stir vigorously for quite some time. Once the concoction has the consistency of cream, salt and pepper to taste. Sometimes mint is added. If you use water to make the *lassi*, ice cubes may be tossed into the drink after blending has occurred. Sip and enjoy.

On His Own

"The spirit wants to drink a salty *lassi*," Nanak says to the dudh-wallah, giving the man some coins.

"And how does the spirit like its *lassi?*" Wrinkles cover the man's face, winding under his chin, down his neck, and beneath his undershirt.

"The same way my mother does." To see over the edge of the counter, Nanak balances on his toes. He smells the creamy milk, yogurt, butter, and wishes he had more coins. "With plenty of pepper and mint," he adds, deepening his voice, puffing out his lips.

A conversation between two men, standing in line behind Nanak, distracts him from the placid smells. He tries to discern if the men have mustaches from the sound of their voices: "No, no, the definition of a slum is a densely-populated area. Which makes all of India a slum. If we are to have Western luxuries, we must learn to live like them, to think like them." No mustache on this man, Nanak thinks. He watches the dudh-wallah spoon yogurt and ice into a cup.

"But all our villages will turn into Kotla with expensive shops run by women who wear saris for the tourists, then go home to put on blue jeans and count their money. Those Western Indians who come back after living over there, they have no sense of family; they're greedy." Nanak stamps footprints into the dusty ground, then rubs them out, deciding that this speaker has a mustache, crinkled and thick. A softness rings the man's voice, as if something hangs in the way of his lips. Closing his eyes, Nanak sees a floating black mustache hung with words that dangle like earrings. *Village, Tourists, Women, Money.*

"Hey, boy, the spirit's beverage." The dudh-wallah hands Nanak a large cup of *lassi* and a small cup of milk. "No charge for yours."

Because he smiles as he drinks, milk dribbles down Nanak's chin. He stands on his toes to place the empty cup on the counter. Glancing back, he is surprised to see that both men have full beards.

The Man-Woman

As the boy steps away from the stall, he almost collides with a woman. She has short black hair, short like a man's. Her lips are scarlet, and she wears black trousers and a grey silk blouse. Nanak stands close enough to her to see an indentation in the side of her nose where once a jewel must have been. She carries a briefcase and shoves at a cotton-candy wallah who presses against her as he walks by, "*Arrey*, asshole, who do you think you are?" Her voice is harsh, outraged. The man regains his balance and purses his lips into an exaggerated kiss, shaking his stick of bagged pink cotton at her. Again, the woman shoves him, her voice now hysterical, "I have a PhD for God's sake, how dare you, how dare you?" The man ducks as the woman swings her briefcase at him. It swoops over Nanak's head, and he drops his cup on the ground. White *lassi*, dotted with black and green flecks, runs over his canvas shoes, pooling near the toes.

When he sees the boy's tears, the dudh-wallah gives him another *lassi* and cup of milk, both free. By the time Nanak leaves the stall for the second time, the woman with short hair is gone. He will ask his auntie about her. A woman with man-hair and man-wrath he has never seen before. She must be possessed by some spirit, he thinks, tightly clenching the new cup of *lassi* between his hands. He takes a sip of the drink, careful to wipe the incriminating white film from the cup's edge, but he forgets to clean his mouth.

What Nanak Will Remember

On the way back to the tomb, the cup of *lassi* between his hands, Nanak looks into an open doorway. He sees an elderly man in a white turban. Above his head, the man holds a small boy by the armpits. They turn together in a circle. Inside the house, the light is blue and glowing. They are laughing, both old man and young boy. Nanak wants to feel the man's hands under his own arms; he wants to swing and laugh. He stops walking, leans against the doorframe, and watches as the man lowers the little boy to the ground. Into the blue light of the house the boy lurches, and Nanak realizes that he limps not from dizziness but because he has a withered leg.

If Nanak had not stopped in the doorway, he would never have known that the boy was lame. He would only have remembered the sound of laughter, and the way the old man cupped the boy's armpits. And if the man had not lifted the boy, had not spun him above the ground, the boy might never have known the ease and smoothness of flight. The image of the man and boy stays with Nanak till he himself is an old bearded man, long after he has forgotten the possession, the screaming women, the spilled *lassi*.

A Second Man-Woman

There is a white woman, an American, inside the tomb now. She sits with her back against the northern brick wall. Like the man-woman from the street, she has short black hair and wears trousers. An orange scarf covers her head and her feet are bare, like everyone else's. Nanak gives the *lassi* to his father and steps over and across and around the howling women to get to the American.

"What type of spirit possesses you?" he asks her. She takes a tissue out of her pocket and wipes the coat of *lassi* from his lips. In Hindi, she replies, "Why do you want to know?" Immediately, he answers with another question, "Are short-haired women possessed by the P-H-D?"

He does not understand why the woman laughs for so long, but he is thrilled by the sound because it reminds him of birds in the morning. When she pats him on the head, he takes a step back, out of reach of her hand, and demands an answer to his question. He repeats, "What type of spirit possesses you?"

Smiling, the woman fidgets with her scarf, pulling tight the knot at the nape of her neck. With her head tilted down, Nanak sees gold threads running horizontally across the cloth. He wants to touch them, and he steps toward the woman, again within reach of her hand.

"What type of spirit possesses me?" the woman asks, tucking the sides of the scarf behind her ears.

She shrugs. "Curiosity, I guess."

Nanak leaves the man-woman, the second he has ever seen, the first he has spoken to. He steps across the bodies till he reaches his mother. Her eyes are rolled back in her head, shivering, and her tongue drips pink blood. "Ma," he says, and reaches for her hand.

The Spirits, Joy and Guilt

My name is Khushi, and I have always lived inside this girl. From her mouth I tumble in loud howls; I flit around her neck and thighs, so she will bounce and toss her head. Poor girl, she stifles me, covers her laughing mouth and slows her skipping. She hangs her head when her mother scolds, "Do your duty, be a good, clean girl and act as you should, not as you feel." But I am perverse and persistent. Sometimes I guide the girl into dusty streets where she and the legless beggars play patty-cake. Other times, I make her run so fast that she trips and sprawls and muddies her *kameez*. And when she is spanked, her mother's hand hard upon her, I tilt her eyes toward the sky. Am I really to blame when she laughs aloud to spite the spanking? The girl, she boils with happiness because she is alive, alive, and the day is not yet finished. This Thursday, she and I have come to the tomb. First, she lies down and laughs raucously till she chokes. Then she spins and drums among the people, unwinding turbans, whooping, clapping her hands, dancing wildly till she falls in a most unladylike way. With her hands on her hips, she says, "I will act as I feel, not as I should. I am happy! Why must I hide?"

My name is Pathak, and I am new to this old woman. She was walking by the tomb, just a few minutes ago, when the tip of her cane gouged me from the earth. As a vibration, I climbed the cane, then twirled into her withered hand. Up the white marble stairs she hobbled, past the tomb, into the brick courtyard. She stood in the doorway, looking upon the women, the men, the children, and she whispered, "I am sorry for the cruel things I have done." When she spoke these words, I swept from her. I called to the spirit, Pyaar, love, who was watching a man with scratched cheeks, his wife, and their boy. I asked Pyaar to drift this way, over my old woman. And so he did.

Friday Comes

After a full day and night of possession, Apsara is tired. Gopal has promised more than seventeen times that he will stop drinking whiskey, and Nanak has been napping in between the errands run for the spirit's great appetite. The white woman did not stay long at the tomb; she sleeps alone in a hotel bed under a rotating fan. Across the city, Farouk is just awakening and deciding to nest under the blankets for a few more minutes. And there, over Apsara's head, hangs a pale yellow cloud of smoke, signifying the departure of the pure spirit.

Nanak, the shoe-finder, locates his green shoes and those of his parents. He carries a sack stuffed with the spirit's new kitchenware. The family is delayed from leaving the tomb because others also want the boy to find their footwear. A large crowd gathers around Nanak, but when Apsara grunts impatiently, Gopal ushers her and the boy down the white marble steps, past the *lassi* stall, along three busy avenues jammed with traffic, and out to the city's edge where their two-story house stands on a small plot of land.

As they close the front door behind them, Auntie rumbles up in a bicycle rickshaw. The rickshaw-wallah is skinny. He stands on his pedals, throwing the weight of his slight body behind the circular motion of his legs, forcing them to work down and around, down and around. His arms shake from exertion, his chest heaves, his breathing sounds like a hacking cough. Even the bicycle, wobbling wheels and taut chain, strains under the burden of Auntie's body and her two big trunks.

After helping her down, the rickshaw-wallah hoists Auntie's trunks, one at a time, onto his back and carries them to the front door. She gives him a meager tip, and he grumbles, "Thank you, lady; your generosity is as bounteous as your body." Since she is already pounding on the door and calling for her young nephew to come and help her, she does not hear what he says.

That night, at dinner, the rickshaw-wallah tells his four children about Auntie and her tremendous trunks. When they laugh at the way he tells the story, he is pleased.

Twang
(Release)

My mother taught me to hunt. "Daughter," she said, "women kill," and so it was. If I clenched my legs by sinew and muscle, I moved soundless through the birch. My mother and I, we stalked, we stole, our strikes merciful and accurate. The bowstring hewed a deep furrow in my index finger. When I pressed my ear to their cool white trunks, the birch told me where to go to find rabbit for stew, squirrel for pie. They have always spoken to me, the trees.

Before I was born, my mother cleared a space among the birch and built a roofless house of stone. We had ivy for carpet, red foxes for pillows when we could catch them. As we slept, the foxes gnawed on our heads. Their rough tongues scrubbed our cheeks. Fox-tail smells of home, red and gold. If you catch a fox, smell, and you'll see what I mean. But do not try too hard; they have grown shy and quick.

In fall, the ivy turned from green to orange and slipped like a flame across the floor of our house. At the corners of our walls, birds made their round, twiggy nests and hunted the insects humming in the ivy. I liked how the baby sparrows clamored for food: blind, demanding. My mother and I gathered molted feathers to fletch the end of our arrows, to steady their flight.

When the other woman came to join us, she built a roof of pine trunks fitted so neatly together no light splashed through. The ivy browned, then died. The foxes bit deep into our arms and scrabbled to be free, barking. Before the woman came, there was no need for me to have any will. But after—such a sharp slap of a word, *after*—my will sprouted. Because I needed it. That year, the birch that had been a seed when I was born turned ten.

She had a hidden face tucked into shiny, red humps of skin. My mother found her pretty. Always the woman whispered, so that my mother leaned close into her, so that I could not hear what she said. The woman filled the house with lifeless things. Sturdy, immovable dressers, wool rugs of constant colors, paintings of birches. Paintings

Twang (Release)

of birches! The house surrounded by lithe, whistling trees, but she stayed inside and looked at paintings. She told my mother that as I grew older I would want to leave and find a man, and my mother would be alone again. In a creeping fashion, she made herself indispensable.

Oh, she was useful, unfailingly dependable. That woman could do anything. Cook, clean, stitch a sofa, carve a table. First, it happened to my mother. Her will wilted. Gradually, she did less. A haze drifted over her. She lounged on her side, her lean arm a pillow, and the woman bustled around her. And when I looked at my mother, I no longer recognized her. She sent me out to hunt. By myself. I did not like feeding that woman, but I did as my mother asked.

One day, my mother roused herself and left the house to gather sage. The woman and I were alone together. I stood next to her as she kneaded dough. She had built a kitchen, forged a stove, fashioned a countertop. On that countertop, she pounded the dough. Moving, like a streak of wind, she sprinkled flour on her fingers and the lump of raw bread. Occasionally, she glanced at me, her eyes flat and glassy. I had never seen a fish, never hunted one, but somehow I knew she shared their eyes.

Lifting the dough, she slammed it onto the counter. Spores of flour rose and hung between us. Turning the dough, she dug the soft pads of her fingers into its sticky flesh. A heaviness settled upon me. She would take care of everything. I need not do; I need not move. My mother, I knew, waded among the sunflowers at the edge of our plot. All their faces turned toward the house. The light fell there, in the space she had cleared, and the sunflowers strained toward it. I thought of my mother parting the flowers, disappearing into the birch. She sniffed the air for sage, her face upturned. Before the woman, we had sniffed together.

When the bread was done, the woman took it from the oven and placed it on the counter. "Eat," she said to me. Her eyes flew at me, stuck. My stomach hardened. Firmly, my teeth settled into each other.

"No," I said. We faced each other over the bread, a sweet steam rising from its surface erupting with edges of nuts and raisins. I smelled chocolate, too. Cluttered, I thought. She cluttered the bread.

The woman sliced the loaf into thick slabs. She pushed a piece under my nose. "Eat," she said again. I shook my head. No. I would not eat.

"Bread is good for you," she wheedled. "You like it. You want to eat this slice. It will feel soothing, huddled in your stomach." Left then right, she tilted the bread. "No," I said, but I did not move away from the proffered food.

Twang (Release)

Something strong and blood-flavored rose inside me. It filled me.

She lowered the slab and wrenched raisins and nuts from it, a chocolate goo coating her fingers. The chips had melted and spread through the arteries of the dough. We stared at each other, over the cooling bread. And so we stayed till my mother returned with sprigs of sage sticking from her pockets. I had won. My will overpowered the woman's. She pitted her strength against me, and I knocked it aside with my own.

The second time my mother left the house, this time without stating why, the woman and I battled again. I watched from the doorway as she hacked down five sunflowers, taller than her by a yard. She cut with spite, I think because the flowers had no use for her. When she came inside, dragging the flowers behind her like hunting spoil, she laid them at my feet. She filled five huge canning jars with water and lined them up before me.

Taking tubes of dye from her apron, she squeezed drops into each jar. The drops fell to the base of the water, then unfurled and rose like smoke through the liquid, changing it. In the end, there were five containers filled with green, red, black, blue, and orange water.

"Put one flower in each jar," she commanded. I allowed my knees to buckle, and I sank to the floor. I sat on my hands and looked up at her. In response, she smiled, then grabbed each flower by the neck and thrust it into a jar. She ran out of the house, and I fell asleep with my hand on my bow.

That woman, she did not come back till nightfall. And when she stood in front of me, in front of the flowers, I knew she was angry.

"You could not find my mother?" I asked. "Maybe she has left you."

Pointing to the flowers, she said, "Look at them. Your sunflowers are not yellow."

Each one had turned the color of the water it floated in. Green, red, black, blue, and orange.

I laughed then, for it was a mean and stupid trick. "You cannot change the dozens around the house," I said. The smell of the pine roof turned my stomach. But I was pleased to see that the tips of the petals had retained their given pigment. I hoped she noticed, too.

After that day, the woman would not speak to me. My mother never came home, and the woman, she never left. We lived in silence. The colored sunflowers and their water dried up. Neither of us moved the jars. They stood as a line between us. She stayed on one side, in the kitchen. She baked and blew about. Still windlike, she was, but I could hear a hint of moan in her movements. I stayed on the other side of the jars, near the door, so I could come and go as I pleased.

Early one spring, I stood on the husks of sunflowers and examined the birch. I could feel seeds gathering beneath my feet. Soon they would push, green and stubby, through the soil. A black squirrel darted in front of me, followed closely by a red one. They chased each other up trees, they rolled and nipped. Small branches crashed down and thunked against the roof. The woman came outside and stood next to me.

"They're trying to kill each other," I said, not looking at her.

The woman laughed. She watched the squirrels and said, her voice raspy with years of silence: "They're loving each other. It's spring and they want to be together."

"That can't be love," I said, disbelieving.

"It is," she murmured, and wiped her hands on her black apron.

Later that night, the woman made soup for me. Good and warm, clear and mushroomy. "It's nice with croutons, go on, try it," she said, and I did, to please her. She struck a match and I cupped my hand around it. Carefully, to create less wind, we moved in unison toward a candle. Both of us knew that we lit it for my mother, but neither of us spoke this aloud. My mother, my mother: gone.

Where the Long Grass Bends

The next morning, we were back to our old ways. But we did not fall silent ever again. I am grateful for that day of peace. Had those moments of forgiveness not passed between us, I might have felt guilty about her death.

That woman, she died in the only way possible for her. In a great wind, a hurricane. After all, only wind can extinguish wind. I climbed into the root cellar, calling for the woman to join me. But she wouldn't. She said she would not let a storm drive her from *her house* (how I hated her, when she said that). As I pulled the trapdoor shut behind me, I saw her for the last time. Standing in the slanted rain and diagonal wind, she stared up at the sky. In the midst of all that power, she seemed a puff, a brief exhalation. I admired her stubbornness, despite its folly. Me, I sat in the dark hole, the smell of earth, onions, potatoes, and carrots, lulling me to sleep.

Since my mother and I had dug the root cellar at the edge of the sunflower patch, I heard the roof collapsing only as a low and unfamiliar thud. In retrospect, I recognize the moment of the woman's death.

The pine roof snapped at the apex and tumbled into the house, burying the woman, the carpets, the shelves and dressers. Afterward, only one of her hands was visible, white and clutching. The hand was twisted in such a way that I could not tell if it was attached to her right or left arm. A girth of pine trunks covered the rest of her. Over the hand, I said: "Good-bye, woman." I was surprised to feel so alone.

Although all the flowers and young birch had been uprooted and destroyed, it was satisfying to see my house, the house my mother built, returned to its original state. Roofless and open to the sky. The dead sunflowers stank as they decomposed. That smell will always remind me of hurricanes, be they wind or woman. These days, the pine trunks have rotted, and ivy once again covers the floor, forming strange bumps where it creeps over the broken remains of stove and sofa. Sparrows roost at the corners of the house, but the foxes, they never returned.

I went into the birch carrying a small sack of food. For weeks I wandered, sleeping in piles of dry leaves, eating the carrots, onions, and potatoes from the root cellar. Once, I stopped to make a bow and arrow, but upon completing the weapon, I threw it aside. I did not have the heart to kill rabbits. The woods were ragged from the storm, leaving animals no place to hide. Even the sun seemed fierce, with nothing to block it.

Finally, I reached the edge of the birch. Then I was very afraid. It had never occurred to me that the birch could end, would end. I believed them to stretch on forever, like the sky. I turned nineteen that day. And on that day, I met the man who called me willful.

He was tall and bowlegged and his shirt was red. The heel of his left boot was ground down, flattened. Walking with a gentle roll, from side to side, he relied too much on his left leg. Later, I would realize he was wavelike. Later, he would show me his collection of left boots, stored in a cabana by the seashore. One hundred and thirty-five boots, all brown. "I like brown," he said, when I asked him why he didn't try a different color. He had never replaced a right boot, but every three months, he changed the left.

He called me willful because I would not laugh at him. To me, he wasn't funny. This he found incomprehensible. "I am a comedian," he said, "I have to make you laugh." He told me jokes about people I did not know, of Jew and Polack, St. Peter and some gates. "Why is any of this funny?" I asked him. Then he called me willful, and asked me if I had ever seen the ocean. "No," I told him, "but I knew a woman who had eyes like a fish."

"Good," he said. "You'll come with me then."

As we walked toward the ocean (he claimed it was twenty-five miles away), he asked me many questions. After the fifth mile, he told me that in addition to being willful, I was half-crazy and had been born without a sense of humor. I said that perhaps humor had to do with place and what a person was used to. I asked him if he had ever found crows funny when they waddled around a carcass. Or a stream reforming itself around a rock. Or his mother while she peacefully snored a tune. When he said no, I told him all of those things made me laugh. He shrugged.

There was a song he sang to me. The only part I remember is, "...and she feeds you tea and oranges that come all the way from China, and just when you want to tell her that you have no love to give her, she gets you on her wavelength, and lets the river answer that you'll always be her lover." It was a sad song, but he laughed at the end of it. He told me that large audiences scared him so he was not a successful comedian. I had never been in a room with more than two other people. When I saw the ocean for the first time, I thought of the word he had taught me: *audience*. So big that it frightens. The birch seemed shrunken and distant to me then.

We came to the boot cabana first. It was night, so I could not see the ocean, only hear and smell it. From that, though, I knew its might. It bellowed.

The cabana smelled like old, dead rabbits. Sideways, the man smiled and said, "See how I wore those left boots out. See how they rest in their grave by the sea." For an instant, I hesitated. Maybe he was not a good man. But besides the windy woman, he was the only person I had ever met, and so I stayed. I do not count my mother as a person I have met because she seems to be a part of me, someone who was always there, someone who will always remain.

That night, I slept behind the cabana, a brown left-boot for my pillow. At first, the sound of the ocean kept me awake, and I thought about my mother. She had seen the sea; she had come across it as a child. "That makes you a Narrowback," she said. I remembered a story she told me, one day, as we hunted in the birch. "Let me tell you about how the Irishman got the soup," she said. We crawled on our bellies toward a nervous grey squirrel. At the sound of her voice, the squirrel scurried away, but we didn't care. Sometimes while hunting, we purposefully misshot an arrow or misthrew a rock.

When my mother told a story, I lived it. Under a net of branches, she began: "Once there was an Irishman who left home and went to America by boat." The forest floor suddenly pitched beneath me. I smelled salt; I heard the creak of wood, the whip of sail.

"When the boat got to America, it stopped at a small island. The Irishman was sent to a hospital where he lay in bed for weeks. Every day a nurse came and fed him soup." Tasting gritty barley, I smacked my lips. Soup. My mother did not describe the nurse, but I saw her—pale, with a green vein running from the top of her forehead to the scoop between her eyes.

"One day the Irishman did not feel like eating so he gave the soup, untouched, back to the nurse. She coaxed and threatened him, but still he refused to eat. Finally she left. But she returned that night to give him an enema that the doctor had ordered.

"The next day, another man was placed in the bed next to the Irishman. 'How do they treat you here?' he asked. 'Well,' the Irishman said, turning on his side, 'They're pretty good. But make sure you eat the soup, because if you don't you'll get it anyway, right up the arse.'"

At the end of the story, my mother laughed and laughed. I saw inside her: the arch of pink throat, canyons of molars. "Life is like that, Aileen," my mother said. "Sometimes you get things you don't want." She turned away from me, but I knew she was crying.

I had never met a man but often read about them. My mother gave me biology books so I could learn their funny anatomy. It pleased me to discover that water makes up ninety-eight percent of human bodies. When I asked about my father, my mother said she had known him for one year. She said I had his brown eyes and soft skin. He was from a place called Brazil, and before he left, he gave my mother a jade ring. I wear it now, on my thumb.

Where the Long Grass Bends

The man who called me willful was the first real male I knew. For someone who wanted to make others laugh, he was very somber. I wondered if all men were like him. Or maybe just comedians.

While it was still dark, the man woke me. "Time to get to the boat," he whispered, although there was no one to hear us except the surf. We walked another three miles, following the water as it funneled into two spits, two arms of land. The closer the arms drew to each other, the calmer the water in between. How soothing my mother's arms had felt. I wanted to be embraced and pacified, like the water. I walked closer to the man, admiring his thick hair and curvy lips. Steering me, he put his hand on my back.

We reached a harbor filled with quiet, rocking ships. Light fell on the water in washboard shapes. The man said, "We have to be careful. Some people get uptight if they see me near the boats." When he said this, I slipped into my hunting legs. He was surprised by how soundlessly I moved. Once, he lost me even though I stood right next to him. When I touched his shoulder to let him know where I was, he grabbed and shook me. "Stop making a fool of me," he growled. I almost turned and erased myself into the darkness, but the sight of the boats and the idea of getting on one was exciting.

Twang (Release)

The boat we borrowed was about twenty feet long and had a motor. It was loud and created vibrations that thrummed up my legs into my stomach. I wanted to examine the motor, but did not want the man to know it was unfamiliar to me. "Sit up front," he ordered, and slapped his hand on a red padded seat. We set off. Even more than the boat, the red seat indicated adventure.

To our left hung a slip of moon, strap of stars. To our right, a streamer of pink dawn showed. And so, in the middle of night and day, up the channel of water, we puttered. The farther away the harbor, the wider the distance between the two arms of land. I felt released, let go.

After a while the land disappeared, and it seemed that we cut through the center of the ocean. Gradually, the pink dawn deepened to red and tinted the tips of the waves. The water curled and sank. It grew up, up, and out; five-foot swells lifted and dropped the boat, as if it were a toy. And all around, the glinting sea, the marcelled waves. I left my seat and leaned over the side of the boat, enjoying the spray foaming against my cheeks, rinsing my eyes. Faster, the man drove, and the motor churned strongly under my feet. At times, the little boat soared up, and I felt as if I would float away. But the waves slammed the boat down again, rattling my teeth, pushing me deep inside ribs and against spine. The sun climbed; the foam turned sapphire. The motor droned over the slam and suck of waves; water shone on my forehead. Wind drenched me, blasted and snapped. I was happy. And still, all around us stretched the sea.

The will of the ocean crept up on me. As I looked at the water, it occurred to me that there was nothing else to see. Even the sky seemed like a type of ocean, only dry. I was adrift, lost. All this water—the same stuff that filled me. Staring into the chop, I suddenly felt as if my body had sprung a leak. What was inside me was also all around. Was I now empty?

Two hours had passed. The man watched me. "You look green," he said. "You're probably seasick." He smiled; he rolled from side to side effortlessly, communing with the sea, its dips and crests. He was beautiful.

I noticed that I had not moved in some time. I noticed that I sat on the floor of the boat. To myself, I said, "Raise your hands to your head," but they would not lift. I flopped about. The sea so big; me, so small. It made me angry, that water stealing my will. Standing, I faced the ocean and locked my knees. Twice I fell to the deck because the waves wanted me there. Both times I forced myself to stand again. The weighted will-less feeling bore down on my back. Really, I wanted to lie down, to be rocked and pummeled by a force stronger than my own. I found my weakness strangely relieving.

"You're seasick," the man scolded after I had fallen for

Twang (Release)

the sixth time. "Kneel and turn toward the water. Don't make a mess in here."

I rested my head on the gunwale of the boat. If I looked out to sea, my mind whirled. My eyes closed although I willed them open; they loathed the sight of the ocean. Faced with that infinity, they simply refused to see.

The man began driving the boat in tight circles. He seemed to think this would improve my condition. It didn't. For hours, I was sick over the side of the boat. But when I slept it was with one hand dangling in the cold water to let the ocean know I was still there; I had not given up. Once, I awakened to sharp bites on my fingers. The ocean was still there, too.

My seasickness lasted ninety days. An ingenious capacity for change—that was my foe, the ocean. As soon as I grew accustomed to one motion, another took its place. The man enjoyed taking care of me, peeling oranges, squeezing pits from the fibrous seams and cloudy skin. In the beginning, fruit was all I could stomach. He wiped my mouth and rubbed my back; he carried me to the edge of the boat and dipped my feet in the water. Twice a day, he dangled oranges a few feet from where I lay so I had to crawl to eat. If he had not done this, I wouldn't have moved at all. Sometimes he sang to me. He had a beautiful voice, like the sea on a wild, choppy day.

Where the Long Grass Bends

When we ran out of gas, we floated. There was fresh water and canned food stored in the hull of the boat. Surviving on syrupy pears, tuna, Spam, crackers, and olives did not bother me or the man. After the first month, I ate voraciously.

We slept under a maze of stars. One night, the man pulled me against his chest and sang about a place called Mississippi Goddam and having the right to sing the blues. The tunes warbled behind his breastbone, wordless and deep. When he sang, his face changed. He was a different person, someone smaller, softer. Afterward, he pressed his lips against mine. My jaw muscles cramped with a curious blend of hurt and want, like they had when, as a child, I ate lemons. Every night, the man pressed something else of his against me. I thought of lemons and their thick dented skins. In the birch, I had used my teeth to rake the sour pulp away from the rind. I did the same to the man's body, with less force. He liked it. I could tell from the way he subsided.

I asked the man to tell me the name of every fish we saw, of every constellation and piece of kelp. There was one element he could not name. A phosphorescence that appeared as darting spots, just under the waves, always in the morning. When I asked him what it was, he answered, "I don't know." Something inside of me leaped. I loved that unnamed glow, that thing that would not be known. Every night, before we went to sleep, the man said to me, "I do not love you; I have nothing to give." I nodded and smiled.

By the end of the third month, my will returned. I, too, could stand and roll with the waves. I learned not to fight the ocean, but to let the water inside me float freely. I twinned my insides to the sea. I enjoyed the ocean's span; I enjoyed it as an audience. It was then the man and I fought.

He told me unending jokes; there was no place to hide. Once I even jumped into the water to escape him, but he dragged me back to the boat by my hair. "You'll stay with me," he said. "Or I'll grind you down like a left boot." One thing I knew about my will was that uncontested, it slackened. With someone to fight, it grew bold.

Without warning, in the fifth month, the man lost his will. Awakening, I was ready for battle. But all day he lay on his side with his eyes closed and murmured softly to himself. "My right heel is flattening," he said. "I don't want to go back, they won't laugh at me, they won't like my jokes." It was not the sea that caused his will to sicken, nor was it me. Something inside of him slumped, something he could not see or name. Not knowing what else to do, I watched him and forced peaches and tuna down his throat. Before I lay down beside him to sleep, I asked him to tell me that he did not love me or have anything to give. He stayed silent. So I said it for him. "You do not love me; you have nothing to give." Usually this made him cry. Fifteen hours a day he slept. Nothing I did affected him. His will was entirely gone.

One night, as the man slept, I pinned his body under my own. Holding his nose closed, I pried open his mouth and breathed into him. With my air, I gave him will. Like waves, his chest rose and fell. Rushing out of me, into him, my breath.

When the sun shone down on us, he sat up, gleeful. I had expected myself to weaken with each breath I gave. But I felt fortified. So did he. He embraced me, saying I had saved him. He called me a saint, a treasure, and sang a song called "Fine and Mellow." With confidence, he cracked jokes, striding up and down the length of the boat, his boots sounding like vigorous surf. Often I would find him gazing foolishly at me. When he told me "I do not love you; I have nothing to give," I did not believe him.

On a rainy morning, the man said it was time to go back to land because we were almost out of food. He removed two massive oars from the hull of the boat—one for me, one for him—and we began to row. After seven days we sighted land, off to the south. All those months, we had traveled no more than forty miles into the ocean, then drifted about in a large, messy circle. When I saw that trim shoreline, I felt close to the man. I wanted to be with him

Twang (Release)

always. "Today, the foam takes the shape of a bride," he said, grasping me jealously around the waist. Nodding, I felt sure of our future. I told him how home smelled red and gold, like fox tail.

We arrived back at the same harbor we had left from. There were the quiet, rocking ships. Dawn lingered on the horizon, a pink flush. I felt as though everything had changed. The man docked the boat but did not secure it, and I put the last can of peaches in my pocket before jumping onto land. I was ready to go where the man asked, ready to put my will aside. Placing his hand flat against my chest, he smiled. "Aileen," he said. "I do not love you; I have nothing to give." And then he turned and ran.

I chased him, following those run-down boot prints. He shouted at me, "I don't love you! Leave me alone!" and hid like a squirrel in trees and bushes. The trees, they remembered me, and told me where to find him. If I asked nicely, they allowed me to carve messages into their trunks: *"Love is an act of will. You will love me. You will."* Still the man ran, shouting his message: "I don't love you; leave me alone!" I never heard him, because I didn't want to.

When he reached the birch, I stopped chasing and watched him dart into the woods. His red shirt flashed between the white trunks; his boots thudded on the leaf-strewn ground. I knew what I had to do.

Cross-legged and with my back against a tree, I made a bow and twenty-five arrows.

For shafts, I used willows. Striking quartz against slate, I whittled stone points. Twined hanks of my own hair served as string. And a young yew branch, curved by the pressure of my hair tied at either end, formed a bow. I caught a seagull and plucked it to feather my arrows.

With the weapon finished, I gathered red berries and stained my face in fat stripes. I wove a belt of poison ivy and ate the can of peaches for strength. Then I went into the birch, following the man's clear tracks at a run.

I found him just where the trees said he would be. He was standing, leaning against an old birch. From ten feet away, I notched my arrow and took aim. He heard the whine of the bow and snapped his head up. That twang and release, the arrow's thin speed. I thought of my mother as she threw rocks into trees, warning chipmunks, so they could escape her. Tasting blood, my body filled and swelled. I willed that arrow to its mark.

It sank into the edge of the man's shirt, pinning his right arm to the tree. Around the arrowhead, the cloth wrinkled. The man opened his eyes and looked at the willow-shaft. When he moved his left hand toward it, I loosed another arrow, forcing both of his arms into stillness. With twenty-five arrows, I fastened his shirt and pants to the birch. I shot two arrows into the pointed toes of his boots, and rooted him to the ground.

"Aileen," he said, as I crawled on my belly and elbows toward him. "You've gone crazy. I told you all along that I don't love you; I have nothing to give. You refused to hear me."

"Will yourself to love me," I said, rising to stand in front of him. He looked like a porcupine, quilled and defensive.

"I can't," he said. "I won't."

"Why not?" I stamped my foot.

"I don't know," he replied. "You'll just have to let me go."

My will surged and blood beat against my ears. I felt sure they were turning red. Until he agreed to love me, I would keep him pinned to the tree. Folding my arms, I sat down at his feet and looked up at him. He seemed to know my plan and sighed. I sensed a joke coming.

"Did I ever tell you the story of how the Irishman got the soup?" he asked.

Was that a whip of sail? I closed my eyes and felt the roll of the sea. I saw my mother's arch of throat, heard her tight laugh. The underside of the man's chin hung soft and sallow. I used my hands to push off the ground. I stood.

From the sleeve of his left arm, I removed three arrows. "You can get free now," I said and walked into the birch, leaving my bow on the ground. The next day, I was back inside my mother's house.

"Life is like that, Aileen," she had said. "Sometimes you get things you don't want." What if she had reversed the words, an alteration, here, then there? Life is like that, Aileen. Sometimes you don't get the things you want. Are the meanings the same? Is there any difference? I don't know.

Those were his words: *I don't know.* One day, at sea, the man asked me if I prayed. I said no, but I think about how to be good, to do good; I think about keeping my will strong so I do not get something I don't want. Never had I thought to rearrange my mother's words. I had not foreseen the day when I would squelch my own will and lose the thing I wanted.

A week later, I went back to that old birch. I did not expect to find the man still pinned to the tree, but I knew something of him would remain. His boots were there, rooted to the ground. He must have slipped from them, leaving the woods in socks so I could not track him. It had wounded him to leave the right boot, that I was sure of. Searching for my bow, I found a squirrel's cache of nuts and filled my pockets. Both boots I carried home with me. I imagined the man walking through the woods, my bow slung over his shoulder, thinking of me.

Twang (Release)

And so I returned to the birch, but not alone, to live in my mother's house. My daughter curled inside me then, a wad, a bundle. Already she can eat with both her right and left hands. When she is older, I will tell her about the sea. I will string a bow for her and feel pride in her straight back. Maybe she will lure squirrels into her arms; maybe she will take pity on the rabbits. I don't know. But I know to teach her to wield a strong will, and I know to teach her to let go. That is enough for a beginning.

The
Excrement
Man

It was the birthing flies on mangoes that drove him away, although she blamed the monkeys who stole his *chappals* and tossed them back and forth across the Bodhi trees.

She named him Bandar, after the old temple monkey. With one blue eye, one brown, and a white forelock, Bandar was born in the middle of the rains when the streets ran with water and shit floated around the cow's knees. The doctor claimed the boy came into the world with a lock of white hair due to the extraordinary age of the father, who at ninety-two did nothing but lie in bed, waiting for his young wife. The astrologer said Bandar's two-color eyes signified his future as a torn man. And the cook, who had been with the family for fifteen years, left, saying the old baby brought misfortune to the kitchen and dulled all the silver pots. Most who encountered Bandar assumed the cook's attitude. Like the monkeys he was named for, Bandar took to crying and swatting with pebble fists. He would fall asleep only if his sister hung his cradle from the Bodhi tree.

At first, it offended Bandar's mother that he would not sleep at her breast. Then she became afraid the monkeys would steal him, but they ignored the baby. Night after night, alone, Bandar swayed in the garden. And so he began his life as a young-old beast-boy, hanging in a tree, with monkeys chattering above his head.

Because of his older sister Somna, Bandar did not walk till age seven. Born asleep with a huge head of black hair, Somna snored through the first three days of her life and crawled on the fourth. As she aged, she ran everywhere. If she stopped long enough for sweat to pool on her tamarind skin, she fell asleep. She hibernated through the rainy season, locked in her room so she would not drown. When the sun finally dried the mildew out of the curtains, Somna rose, ten pounds heavier, and ran through town with the frenzy of one returned from the gods.

When Bandar was two years old, Somna used one of her mother's *dupattas* to strap him with his chest to her chest. She tried strapping Bandar to her back so he could watch where they traveled, but he seemed to enjoy viewing the world in reverse and seeing what Somna could not.

The four main streets of town converged into a square named Char Minar, flanked on all sides by tall thin minarets. The Muslims lived around the edges of the square and ran the market teeming at its center. Every dawn, old men scattered seed for pigeons so prayers for sick wives and sad children would reach heaven in the stomachs of the birds. The muezzins called to the devoted. The chai wallahs began their rounds, wrapped in wool scarves against the morning chill. Smelling of *attar* and meat, the Muslim women bargained roughly with the lace merchants.

The day the temple-monkey died in front of the lingam with a fistful of marigolds in its paw, Somna strapped Bandar to her chest and ran to the market. Over his sister's back, Bandar watched the Char Minar women haggling and hocking streams of *paan* onto the ground. When they raised their arms to strike the gypsies on the head for selling chickens at exorbitant fees, he saw from their red-painted palms down to their elbows. Bandar thought they were the most beautiful women in town. He saw an uncovered girl and her shrouded mother palpating *moulies* at the vegetable stand. He thought that as the girl grew taller, red paint would appear on her palms, and a black chiddor would sprout from her head.

Somna stopped running to watch a vendor ladle oil from a vat into slender-necked jars. She toppled forward and fell asleep. The chai wallahs, the lithograph boy, the bangle hawkers, all laughed and stood up for a better view of the sleeping Somna and struggling Bandar, pinned beneath his sister. The uncovered girl ran over with a *moulie* and tried to prod Somna awake. She smiled at Bandar, and he saw that she had a chipped front tooth.

The girl was named Mez because she was born on a table in the middle of the market. She was almost deaf. She took an immediate liking to the girl who slept like the dead, and the old boy who could not walk but looked at her with great urgency from two different colored eyes.

Twelve Years Later

Bandar did not like dirt. Of any kind. The kind women stank of, the kind he stank of, the kind the monkeys slung. At the Nataraj Ashram, the rishis told him of their abstinence and how true power lay in the sacs between their legs. Holding that power within them, never sharing it with others or spilling it onto their pillows, made them omnipotent. Bandar remembered the days when his feet did not touch the ground, when they were unsoiled and pure, his sister bearing his weight and gathering dirt in his stead. He remembered his face pressed into her chest and the tight bands of cloth under his thighs, holding him in place. He would not be weak.

His mother thought him ridiculous. Every morning and night, he spent two hours in the bathroom. After washing, he painstakingly swiped his body with imported cotton soaked in iodine. Even after the servant cleaned, Bandar walked around the house with a duster, sweeping the chairs and benches he chose to sit on. He wore English shoes, closed at the tops and back so his feet would stay clean, and refused to be in the sun without an umbrella. His *kharchi* was liberally spent on bottled water (which he sipped through a straw) and pomade. He used the hair-oil to plaster his white forelock in a curl above his blue eye.

The family owned three Ambassadors. There was a driver for each car. Bandar ordered himself to be driven to and from school in the newest vehicle, making nasty faces at his walking classmates. Weekends, his mother sent him to the kitchen to cut onions, trying to force him to cry, to act in a human fashion. But Bandar did not want to cry— not for his mother, not because of an onion. He ran to Mez's house and gave her pieces of cloth snipped from his mother's wedding sari. In return, Mez snuck through the back door of his house and chopped the onions for him.

The members of the household called him *rani,*

queen. His mother put clods of dirt under his sheets then ordered him to bed. While he washed, she concealed herself behind the curtains and shrieked with her young laughter upon his discovery of the muck. In a rage, shaking and cursing, he threw the dirt at his mother, "My shit is too good for you, woman. You are a filthy boar." For that, he woke up with his eyes rimmed in *kajal* and his head circled by a tiara of hot chilis. His mother's servant ordered him to clean the toilet for a week, a job reserved for the sickly *jamadar*, for those who were shadows and worked with feces and the dead.

Unlike his sister and mother, Bandar did not go to the movies. The sight of women, their soft stomachs leaning from their saris, black hair swimming down their backs, disgusted him. He wanted to slap and unravel them, to show them their sickening nakedness that could make him and the rishis powerless. When he visited Char Minar, the rage he felt toward women dulled. The covered Muslims soothed him. In Mez's house (her doorway, marked with the red hand of Fatima), the women revealed themselves for his two-color eyes. Unpinning their veils, they made him forbidden beef treats. He loved the unmasked planes of their cheeks, the dents in their chins. Mez's house was a fortress of women. They bared themselves and cursed with relish; they had no servants and cooked for each other.

The Excrement Man

Four hundred miles northeast of town, Mez's father drove a tonga in Delhi. He had lost his job as a market vendor. Years ago, he had crossed the river at its widest point, with seventeen pounds of salt in the panniers on his donkey's back. The waters had been rough, the crossing slow, and most of the salt dissolved. Of course, the salt vendor fired him, and word spread quickly through Char Minar that the man was an unlucky fool. Even so, the flour vendor offered him a job. Mez's father crossed the river at its widest point with ten pounds of flour on his donkey's back. The donkey became so weighed down by the wet flour that he sank underwater and nearly drowned. Mez's father was seen beating the donkey and screaming, "You thought your load was going to get lighter this time, too? I showed you, didn't I. Who is the master now?" After that, no one in town would give him a job. He left the day Bandar's father died at age ninety-eight, the day Bandar's mother refused to don a white sari. Her servant drove her to Bombay where she purchased twenty gold bangles and three French hats.

At school, Bandar learned English. He tried to teach it to Somna while running behind her, but she had no interest in words, and Bandar could not keep pace with her. So he shared the language with Mez. English lacked nuance and was easier for her almost-deaf mouth to mimic.

Where the Long Grass Bends

She read Western magazines and fashioned a dress from scraps of the red wedding sari. Bandar traded her squares, large and small, according to the difficulty of the chore she performed. When the town slept, Mez slipped into her Western dress and ran to the river to look at her reflection.

The night after Bandar's mother missed a club luncheon because he had rewired the phones, he was punished—no dinner and no shower. He ran to the river for solace, cutting through Char Minar and crossing the pea fields. He heard a voice singing the song the Orissa storyteller sang at the end of his sessions:

> My story is done.
> The flowering tree is dead.
> O flowering tree, why did you die?
> The black cow ate me up.
> O black cow, why did you eat the tree?
> The cowherd didn't look after me.
> O cowherd, why didn't you look after the cow?
> The daughter-in-law didn't give me food.
> O daughter-in-law, why didn't you feed the cowherd?
> My little baby was crying.
> O baby, why did you cry?
> The black ant bit me.
> O black ant, why did you bite the baby?

The Excrement Man

I live in the dirt
And when I find soft flesh, I bite.

Platinum, the moon shone that night. The river let Mez admire herself and from behind the scrub trees, Bandar watched her. Everything the rishis told him rushed from his head as Mez uncoiled her hair and smoothed her red dress. She hit a note in her song that no hearing person could make, and Bandar felt his power spilling out of him, down the leg of his dhoti and into his shoe. He watched Mez until she finished her song, braided her hair, and left. Then he took off his shoes and washed himself in the river. Crying weakly, he padded home. His legs quivered, and he felt as if he would die.

As he entered the garden, Somna streaked past. Earlier in the day, crouched by the river, she had watched a water snake swallow a fish. Since then she had not stopped running, afraid that dreams would muddy her memory. When she saw Bandar with no shoes and a wet face, Somna stopped short and fell asleep against the rosebush. Her brother left her there. He crept through the back door, careful to wipe his feet, then tiptoed around the kitchen. He listened to cockroaches scuttling, the drip of the sink. The silver pots repelled moonlight onto the walls. Bandar emptied the contents of his brimming shoe into a

79

glass jar. He sealed the jar and put it in his closet under a pile of freshly starched *kurtas*. Then he climbed into bed, expecting to never awaken.

That night, Bandar dreamt of monkeys. All in red dresses. They fell asleep when he touched them, and he woke drenched in his own sweat and power.

His mother found Somna in the garden. She was talking in her sleep, "Bandar, where are your shoes? Why are you crying? I saw a girl in a red dress. I saw you behind a bush." His mother had the servant put Somna to bed (on account of the approaching rains) and locked her door from the outside. Then she sent the servant to the astrologer's home with a message: later that afternoon, she would come for a visit. Her son needed his chart read since he was due to be married.

What the Stars Said and an Upset Stomach

The astrologer brought Bandar's mother into a room with a fan and mosquito netting, as he did with all women who offered soft gold. He took out his papers and a black fountain pen. He squinted briefly at Bandar's palm before sending him out to the garden. A servant handed Bandar a piece of paper with words scrawled illegibly across it. "A riddle from the astrologer." The servant thumped his chest proudly, "The stars say if I work hard in this house, my son will buy me an auto in my old age."

It took Bandar a half hour to decipher the writing. The words confused him: "What crawls on four in the morning, two in the afternoon, and three at night?" Bandar stared at the paper; still he could make no sense of it. He walked around the outside of the house till he heard the astrologer's shaky voice through an open window. Careful to keep his hands from touching the ground, he squatted under the window to listen.

The astrologer told Bandar's mother that her two-colored son had the Black Spot on his chart, making him unfit for marriage. Any family who saw Bandar's stars would be unlikely to give their daughter to him. In Bandar, Saturn opposed Neptune. He evolved distrustful to a fault, but bountifully generous. His *Rahu* made him adept at business and sensing current trends. He would be helpful to the world, to populations, but not to individuals, not to family or friends. Overly sensitive and meticulous, Bandar's mind and emotions vacillated against themselves. He needed companionship, sought it out, but his inherent nature of withdrawal and finikiness drove away anything soft and good.

Bandar's mother wailed, pounded her fists on the table.

Only the gold on her wrists kept her from true despair. She cried to the astrologer, "My son is a bastard who will never marry, and my daughter cannot stay awake long enough to cook for a man, let alone pleasure him. I am cursed, cursed."

The astrologer tried to calm her with dates from Jaipur and stories of other children who had unfortunate charts. She did not want to be placated. Leaning forward, she pulled the drape of her sari around her head and whispered conspiratorially, "Now tell me, Sahib. Does he *like* women?"

The astrologer leaned back in his seat. "Yes, madam, very much. But he is strange. Why don't you send him to a Christian place? They will know nothing of his chart. On his palm, travel is prominent. You can make that possible, can't you?"

Smiling, Bandar's mother made her fingers into a beak and squeezed two more bangles from her wrist. She pressed them into the astrologer's hand and rose to find her *chappals*. "Thank you, Sahib. You have been very helpful." With his hand on her young back, the astrologer walked Bandar's mother to the garden.

The boy had left the window when he heard his mother mention himself and women. He had discovered a tree, heavy with ripe mangoes, and rigged a slingshot from a stretched-out rubber band and the V of his first two fingers. Taking careful aim, he launched soda caps at the mango stems and ran forward to catch the fruits before they hit the ground and bruised. When his mother and the astrologer found him, Bandar stood beneath the tree, next to a mound of fruit.

"For the monkeys and dogs," he said to his mother. She rolled her eyes.

The astrologer asked Bandar if he had solved the riddle. "It may be a riddle for other men, but not for me," Bandar said, "My riddle is different." Nodding, the astrologer said, "Well then, you know yourself. At least you have that."

On the way home, Bandar's mother asked him if he would like to go to England where they sold his kind of shoes and the food came wrapped in tin and was so bland that no one ever cried from it. He would not answer her. When the driver stopped to let a cow pass, Bandar ran from the car. His mother told the driver to keep going. Bandar lagged further and further behind till she could no longer see him. "To the movies," she ordered, and pressed her head into her knees, whimpering for her children's misfortunes.

When Bandar arrived home, dripping with sweat and disgusted by his own withering smell, he wrestled his mother's servant for the key to Somna's room. The man was very strong. He pushed Bandar to the floor and hissed in the boy's ear, "If you don't leave me alone, you little fag, I will spit in your breakfast every morning." Bandar bit the servant's hand and snatched the key. Opening the door to Somna's room, he locked it from the inside and shook her awake.

"Somna, we must leave after Holi. No one will marry you; you are too sleepy. No one will marry me; I am two-colored. You must make money for us. Go to Char Minar and tell the vendors you will run for them, anywhere they want. I will get some money too, and we will go. We will go where there are no rains and you can run through all seasons. Get up now, and talk to the vendors."

Somna asked him if they had to leave because of the girl in the red dress. He said no. She hung her head and noticed his feet in open *chappals*. "Where are your English shoes, Bandar?"

"They have become soiled," he replied. "I will wear these till we leave. Go now. The vendors know how fast you are."

He went to the kitchen for something to do, troubled and lonesome. There was a basket of mangoes on the countertop. He reached out and took one. Small flies covered the underside of the fruit, overlapping each other in buzzing layers, festering and mating on the skin. Bandar felt dizzy. The dirt of the world settled in his stomach. He vomited on the floor.

Dazed, sickened, he took a jar and scooped some of his bile into it. He brought the jar to his closet and carefully placed it next to the jar filled with his spilled power. Then he walked toward the back door, not knowing where to go, but aware that he needed to be away from the house. As he left, Bandar saw the servant watching from the kitchen, a rag tied around his hand. With his two-color eyes, Bandar looked back at the servant till the man turned, dropped to his knees, and began cleaning the remainder of Bandar's worldly burden off the floor.

Holi and The Hand of Bandar

Bandar and Somna wound their way through Char Minar. Somna blushed when the vendors called out, "Tiger's here, Tiger's here!" She had been running for them, all of them, for six months and had filled five tiffins with crumpled rupees. She hid the tins under her bed. The vendors called her Tiger because of her strength and fleetness; she crossed the river at its widest point with forty pounds of agarbathi, flour, salt, ghee, and lithographs of gods strapped to her front. Even the gypsies paid her to find lost chickens on the plains west of the river. Somna always retrieved the birds, either stiff with death or squawking in protest.

In between Char Minar and the river lay what the

Muslim women called Tikka Street, the only street in town that ran in a straight line and had a beginning and end. In construction, it resembled a long hall, stretching one block between two rows of crowded apartments connected by a stone awning. The awning served as a roof for Tikka Street. The women of the apartments beat their carpets there. Even when deserted, the street was noisy with their pounding.

Two square sheets of cloth hung at either end of the street which kept it dark and cool, a haven at midday. On either side of the street and in perfect symmetry, five small doorways led into rooms eight strides wide. Colored powder filled each chamber, almost to the ceiling. The left side of the street housed blue, green, red, yellow, and orange; the right side, purple, black, white, bright pink, and soft pink. Stationed in each room was a eunuch in charge of selling the powder.

The rich of the town invited eunuchs to perform at weddings. They arrived dressed in garish saris, bedecked in brilliant paste jewels and obscene makeup. They sang in their screechy voices and wreaked havoc on the tabla players, stealing their drums and beating wildly upon them. Clapping with the power of men's arms, the eunuchs were considered more terrifying than entertaining. But a town legend advised that a scorned eunuch would steal a male-child from the offending

86

wedding party and hack off its genitalia. Most believed the eunuchs propagated the legend for their own purposes, but invited them anyway, because one never knew.

The Hindu women of town bought large quantities of powder at Tikka Street, enough for the whole year, and used it to mark their foreheads, make designs, and to ruin the clothes and skin of those they loved—and hated—during Holi. Every year, the first morning of Holi was the busiest and most profitable for the eunuchs. Bandar and Somna spent the entire day purchasing bags of color. It was cold when they left Tikka Street. They saw bonfires and heard cymbals crashing. Walking home under Bandar's umbrella, they both agreed to stain their mother's servant so severely, he would remain multicolored for months. The full moon (it was the night of Phalguna) lit the way home.

The second day of Holi dawned to people laughing and mixing water and colored powder. They poured the concoctions into small pails, pastry dispensers, balloons, goatskin bags. By the time the air warmed, children and adults in their oldest clothes crowded the rooftops of town. No one could ever say who started the color segment of Holi. It was usually a child. That year, some thought Somna began the day; some blamed the gypsies. Either way, the color and powder began flying and the pretty girls fled down dark alleys where they were cornered and soaked till their saris clung to them and bright hues mottled their hair.

From every Hindu roof hung clay *matkas*. Human pyramids strained up toward them. Krishna's favorite curd filled most; others held coins. The mischievous filled theirs with colored water that soaked the stick-bearer and the crowd underneath. Some held nothing at all. When these containers were smashed, the onlookers went into a frenzy, joyfully dousing everything around them, throwing handfuls of powder into the air. Bandar and Somna chased their mother's servant up a tree and bombarded him with balloons containing a myriad of color. When he clambered down, painted with their vengeance, they ran from the garden and ventured into the streets.

Color dripped down the walls of buildings. There was nowhere to hide. During Holi, people became as stealthy as jaguars. For two days, the entire town had precise aim and held no grudges. Bandar and Somna ran to the river where the vendors had erected temporary stalls to sell chai, towels, corn, and rose soap. People meaninglessly scrubbed themselves in the water. As soon as they removed one layer of powder, someone covered them with another. The river was a rainbow. The vendors looked like they had been tortured by the children of cloth dyers. The corn was pink, the tea undrinkable, the towels useless.

The Excrement Man

Bandar had prearranged for his driver to pick him up at the river. He climbed into the backseat of the car and stowed his stained umbrella. He commanded his driver to accelerate as fast as he could and stop for nothing. When they passed a group of people, Bandar flung balloons or emptied a pail of colored water out the window. People chased his car, but he escaped spotless. As the day progressed, there were lulls when it seemed as if the entire town had depleted their color. Inevitably, someone discovered a forgotten bucket, or the resourceful attacked with a volley of green. When darkness finally came, everyone went home to eat, regaling their families with tales of valor.

Bandar went to the river to wash, loathe to see his mother's servant. In case of ambush, he carried a small pail of red water. The moon flickered, trapped behind clouds. As he neared the river, Bandar saw a girl walking in front of him. In the darkness, she looked colorless. Bandar wanted to paint her red. He followed the girl from a short distance and hid himself behind a bush as she waded into the river.

The moon came out and Bandar saw Mez, naked and shivering in the water. She hummed softly and combed out her hair. Bandar forgot himself. He walked to the bank of the river and stared at her firm back, watching goose bumps appear on her skin. He put his pail of red water on the ground and squatted next to it. A stone loosed beneath his foot and plunked into the river.

Mez turned. She saw Bandar sitting next to his pail, his eyes glazed with love. Slowly, she walked out of the river, revealing herself for his two-color eyes. She lay down at his feet, naked, unafraid. He dipped his hands into the pail of red water, then pressed his dyed palms into Mez's flesh, marking her from the neck down. She lay completely still, eyes closed, enjoying the feel of Bandar's hands sticking to her skin.

When she opened her eyes, Bandar was gone and her body bore his handprints—the lines of his destiny stained red on her stomach and thighs. She dressed quickly and ran away from the river, searching the night for him. She ran to his house and entered through the garden gate.

There was Bandar by the swing, digging angrily in the ground. Mez watched as he pulled a silver box from the dirt. He took ten gold bracelets from the box, then reburied it.

She followed him inside and watched from the hall as he packed the bracelets in a small bag. He went to his closet and took two jars from it. After wrapping the jars in *kurtas*, he packed them as well. Then he put the bag under his bed.

Mez stepped into his room. She did not seem to startle Bandar. He looked at her and asked what she wanted.

The Excrement Man

She said, "If you are going away, I will come with you. You have marked me with your hand, with the hand of Bandar, and I cannot go home. They will see me and know it was you, and I will be alone and disgraced."

Impassive, Bandar stared at Mez. He told her she could come with him and Somna, but when they came to a new land where they could rest, she could not rest with him. And she could never ask why.

"I will get my things," Mez said. "Bandar, there is a place I think of. On land, facing sea. When I reach it, I will sit down and say 'I am not leaving here.' I have always thought of it. And you have always been there." She told Bandar she would return at dawn and left the house by way of the garden.

Bandar slept and dreamed of colored monkeys sodden in the rains, of jars filled with his stool stored in a long, narrow room. The eunuchs, wearing red dresses, flitted in and out of the dream. Mez and Somna stood in the rain, ducking dirt and fly-infested mangoes that fell from the sky. In his sleep, Bandar felt a heavy sadness.

When he awakened, it was still dark. After much pulling of Somna's hair, Bandar managed to rouse his sister. He told her to meet him outside. Sleepily, Somna did what he told her, imagining that wherever they went there would be a river and vendors to run for and colored powder. It could not be that different, and Bandar would be there. She, his only sister, would take care of him.

Bandar carried his bag to the garden. He sat and removed his *chappals* to wash his colored feet in the pond. When he reached behind to retrieve his *chappals*, they were gone. He heard a chattering above his head. In the tree that had held his old cradle swing, a monkey, dyed blue and green, chuckled and hopped. It tossed Bandar's shoes to a yellow and red monkey in an adjacent tree. When Bandar tried to climb the tree, the yellow and red monkey smacked him on the head. He cursed at the monkeys. Chattering, they jumped to the tall trees lining the street, gone with his *chappals*. He would have to wear his soiled English shoes.

Bandar cried. The pale sun rose gradually. He heard chai wallahs calling from Char Minar. Turning away from the street, he saw his mother, looking from her window. Watching him cry, in his bare feet. She would remember Bandar, always, like that. He looked at her with his two-colored eyes till she dropped the curtain.

Bandar's stomach cramped in sadness. Running into the street, he squatted and shat across from a cow chewing curd from a broken *matka*. With a banana leaf, Bandar gathered a piece of his own stool and brought it to the kitchen where he pushed it into a jar. He forgot to put on his English shoes. When he returned to the garden, Somna and Mez waited for him. They did not ask him what the jar held or why he wore no shoes. They did not ask him where they were going, hushed by the rainbow streaks on his cheeks.

Before the muezzins called from Char Minar, they left in an oxcart on its way to Thana where the train stopped and the lunatics had an asylum. As they rolled by the river, they saw the shores steeped in color. A flock of pigeons rose above them in a mass, flying west. Somna stayed awake till the town disappeared from view.

A *Christian Place*

After they crossed the ocean and arrived in the Christian place, they passed through a medical station. Bandar was diagnosed with heterochromia and Somna with acute narcolepsy and a fatigue syndrome. When they asked the doctor what the words meant, he told them not to worry, they were not infectious. He told Mez that he had not known her kind of Indian lived across the sea, and registered her as Maize. He forgot to check her ears. Both his eyes were blue and his *a*'s twanged like a sitar.

They left the medical station by boat. On land, they flagged a taxi and Bandar asked the driver to put their things in the boot. The man drove away. They hailed another cab and the driver asked if they would like their things in the trunk. Bandar said yes and learned his first lesson in the Christian place. The taxi took them to a railroad station where they boarded a train going west, intending to stop when they saw a place they liked.

Ten days later, they saw the place. Bandar and Mez poked Somna awake. All she saw was the river, and she nodded her head. As the doors began to shut, they bundled out of the train and found themselves on a platform. In front of them stood a porter surrounded by pigeons. He pointed them up a dirt lane toward a town laid out next to a river. A hill rose beyond the river. All other land in sight was flat.

Some Time Later and a Bad Dinner

No one in town noticed the eunuchs arrive. One day, they appeared, living at the top of the hill in Bandar's long blue house. They did not speak a word of English and only left the house to shop for food. They pointed at what they wanted and held out hands filled with money. Afraid of the eunuchs, the shopkeepers took what was needed and no more.

Bandar designed his home and hired the Christians to build it. He paid them well. The house was shaped like a box, with thirteen windows at the front and back of the top and bottom floors. The Christians tried to convince Bandar to make twelve or fourteen windows, but he would not be dissuaded. One odd window, half the size of the others and asymmetrically placed, looked out the back of the house. It received a full dose of afternoon sun.

A large round bath was sunk into the middle of the ground floor. Everyday, the eunuchs performed ministrations on Bandar. They cleaned, perfumed, dried, waxed, and buffed him, till only his facial hair remained and he smelled of roses. He wanted to be smooth and clean like a baby. In the Christian place, Bandar found it easier to stay spotless and controlled.

Somna was the only woman in the house. Her hibernation cycle had been thrown off by the moderate weather. Instead of running through all seasons, she slept through most. She had grown fat and no longer fit on her bed. Bandar and the eunuchs made her a mattress close to the ground. They turned her every couple of hours, heaving and grunting as they flipped her bulk and changed her diapers. She usually awakened once a week and ran at her old speed down the hill to Mez's house (Bandar had bought it for her with three gold bangles). Rumors spread about the rich, two-colored man who kept an obese woman locked in his house and eighty-seven little dark men in dresses who did whatever he told them. When cows began disappearing from the rancher's herds, they blamed wolves. The people in town heard about it and blamed the eunuchs and the racing fat woman.

During the second year in the Christian place, Bandar invited Mez to the house for dinner. He woke Somna and had the eunuchs walk her around till mealtime. Mez arrived in her red dress with her hair undone and her eyes glazed with love. They talked of Char Minar and Holi and Bandar asked Mez if she needed anything. She told him she wanted a recording device so she could tape her conversations with the people who came to visit her. No one in town knew of her deafness; she had become adept at lip-reading English. But it bothered her that she could not hear the tones of their voices. Bandar agreed to make the machines. He asked Mez how she got along. She told him the people who visited gave her presents of food and other things. She made her own clothing. After attending a quilting session, she became enchanted by the idea of squares of bright fabric sewn into a whole colored piece. She sewed all her clothes in the style of quilts, a stew of color, and gave a few cloaks to Somna who wept and thought of Tikka Street.

Somna felt lost in the Christian place. There were no water snakes in the river, and no one would hire her to run. She tried to lift a statue of their skinny god, the one she thought must be the town favorite because of the number of pictures dedicated to him. She believed she could carry him close to her heart, like the gods on the Char Minar lithographs. But he was so weighted to the earth, she could not even lift one corner of his pedestal. Somna felt sorry for him, stuck to the ground on a cold stone cross. He seemed sad.

She listened to Bandar and Mez talk about the river and the gypsies. She longed for sleep and parcels strapped to her front. She heard Bandar say, "Mez, you were aptly named. You are a table. People come and lay things on you and you hold them up. You are simple and plain, just like a table."

Mez slammed her fists on the table. She had worn her red dress in the hopes that Bandar would remember her. She told him he was aptly named monkey because he looked and acted like one. No one could even tell Bandar was human; he was an unfeeling coward and a homosexual. Then she stormed out of the house, leaving Somna and Bandar alone at the table.

They sat drinking tea and looking in opposite directions till Bandar could tell that his sister was about to fall sleep. He asked her why Mez had left like that, and why she had been so angry. Before Somna's head fell forward onto her empty plate she muttered, "You called her table and you called her plain."

"But that is her name," said Bandar to the sleeping Somna "and she is plain and simple, two very good things."

A few weeks after the dinner, a eunuch brought Mez two recording devices (with written instructions) and an ear horn made by Bandar. She took them, without thanks, and gave the eunuch her red dress to wear.

Maize, the Table

It began with the women. Mez established herself as a seamstress and people flocked to her. They thought she was an American Indian named after corn. The women who came to Mez sat on her sofa and revealed their deepest secrets and problems, without ever realizing that she herself rarely spoke. She offered them sound advice, and did what she could to fix their travails. By the end of her first year in town, Mez knew everyone and everything about them.

She owned a pair of alligator pumps, a gift from the mayor's son. In the process of impregnating the bishop's niece, the mayor's son had left the girl's panties on the back lawn of the rectory. The mayor's son went to Mez on the advice of his mother.

The Excrement Man

The rectory awoke at four-thirty to feed the pigeons and pray. Some time before the birds descended, the panties were retrieved, in a partially frozen state, and delivered to the mayor's son by a eunuch in a red dress. The day after that, the bishop's niece received word from a university in India that her exceptional scholastic ability had reached the attention of the dean, who would be honored to have her attend his school for the next nine months and stay with his childless wife. And the day after that, the ladies at the town restaurant commented on Mez's lovely new alligator pumps.

Mez discovered that she possessed an uncanny talent for invoking trust and solving problems. By the end of her fourth year in town, her home was filled with trinkets, furniture, and paintings. She never paid for food and rarely had to make any; she was swamped with grateful donations and bribes. So accustomed did Mez become to the ways of the Christian place, that she ate their bland food and celebrated Easter.

She sewed one of Bandar's recording devices into the arm of the sofa where she received visitors, and concealed the rotating wheels with a button-up flap. The other recording machine Mez mounted under the kitchen table. After her visitors left, she tied her hair back and listened to the conversations with an ear horn. Their difficulties were resolved soon afterward, unless they had come for the comfort of being listened to, in which case they left fulfilled.

Often, Mez thought of Bandar. Somna visited less and less. Mez longed for some form of real companionship. She still resented Bandar and his insults. The fact that the Christian place accepted her, pleased Mez—she was proud of the life she had created. She liked being needed and dreamt of the day when Bandar would need her, too, as he had years ago when she chopped onions for him and let him touch his hands to her body.

In the Christian place, Bandar became even more withdrawn and solitary. When Mez looked up the hill to his house, she saw that the blue of its facade was slowly fading to grey. The eunuchs told her Bandar bathed three hours each day and frequently told stories about his loving mother and her sweet servant. They feared distance had warped his memory and dulled his color. Mez agreed.

Sometime during Mez's fourth year in town, James came to her. He dismounted the train and asked the porter with pigeons on his shoulders where he could get food and a job. The porter pointed him toward town and told him to find a woman named Maize.

James arrived at Mez's home as she was heating up soup sent over by Grace the Cajun woman who ran the tobacco shop and was known for making food too spicy to consume. After Mez set a place for James at the table, he told her of his adulterous wife whom he had left twelve towns down the train tracks because she did not understand the way he felt. He became so distracted by his own stories that he forgot to eat. Mez silently ate her soup, nodding and watching James' lips. In the middle of an intricate description of his wife's morals, James looked up at Mez. Tears poured from her eyes and coursed into her soup. She lay her head down on the table.

James said, "That's just how I feel."

Mez did not answer because she had not heard him. She got up and took the bowl of untouched soup away from him moaning, "That woman, it's too much."

A flicker of passion took hold of James as Mez moved toward the sink. His passion grew as she coughed. Pushing his chair away from the table, James fled the house, panic-stricken. Mez wept. Oblivious to James' exit, she drank an entire pitcher of water and threw the pot of fiery soup outside the front door, shooing away the cat and cursing Grace and her Cajun pepper.

Days later, Mez received a written marriage proposal from James. Amazed, she listened to the recording of their dinner conversation. She sent a letter back to James inscribed with one word: *yes*. She did not think about his wife or Bandar and his red palms. She wanted to be married. Through the eunuchs, she asked Somna to come to her wedding. When Bandar heard the news, he hugged himself with his thin arms and stamped his feet like a small boy. He knew it was unfair to expect Mez to remain alone, like himself. But he could not help feeling betrayed.

The wedding was a simple affair. The bishop remembered Mez's kindness to his niece and overlooked her heathen status. He married her and James in the church, shuddering every time he glanced at the maid-of-honor. Somna smiled at the skinny god hanging behind the bishop. In her pudgy hands, she clutched bunches of lilies. That night, the bishop rang the bells from midnight till dawn to cover the sounds of Mez's deaf ecstasy. When Grace the Cajun came home from the tobacco store, she found a large bottle of fine brandy and an ornate Venetian bowl on her front step. Inside the bowl was a note: *Thank you for the soup*.

For weeks after the marriage, the bishop could be seen sweating and swinging from the tower with such frequency that the town lost all sense of time. It was impossible to tell if the bell rang for the half hour or for the passion of Mez and James. The couple exhausted each other in this manner till the day James' wife boarded the train and rode twelve towns up the tracks to find a woman named Maize.

She had heard that the Indian lady could do anything from exterminate mice to unearth a long-missing husband. She found her husband on his knees in front of Mez's house, weeding the flower bed. She took him with her to the train station.

Mez returned from her shopping to a half-weeded garden, imprinted with two knee-shapes, and no husband. She did not question his absence. He left her as he had come, unexpected and quick.

In her times of loneliness, Mez would bathe and spank herself with a soup ladle till exhausted. She thought of Bandar, but did not go to see him.

The Storeroom and the Dead Eunuch

On the top floor of Bandar's house was a door with a lock. Behind it was the storeroom. Long and narrow, the room allowed just enough space for a man to walk up and down its length. Jars lined the walls, jars filled with Bandar's stool, save the two brought from India containing his power and worldly burden. Each was labeled accordingly:

> *Mez at the River in a Red Dress*
> *The Mango and the Astrologer*
> *The Day After Holi*

Where the Long Grass Bends

The Day the House Was Built
The Day Somna Was Too Fat for Her Bed
The Day Mez Left Dinner
The Day Mez Married
The Day He Left Mez

When the afternoon sun sloped through the window and gleamed off the jars, Bandar went to the storeroom and thought of his home and Mez by the river. He knew he was less emotional in the Christian place. He had not cried since the day after Holi; he had not spilled his power since the night he dreamed of raining mangoes. The eunuchs' ministrations gave him pleasure because they made him feel smooth like a child free of dirt and sadness. He longed for someone to cradle him, longed for the security of his swing hanging from the Bodhi tree. But he allowed himself no vulnerability, and forced his insides to be still and quiet.

He no longer had Somna as a companion. The year after James left Mez, Somna awakened with her head stuffed full of dreams. She had been asleep for three months and felt hungry and energetic. She ran from her room, tumbling down the stairs in her haste. She never even saw the eunuch.

When Bandar and the other eunuchs finally pulled her off him, he was dead. They burned him behind the house, facing the flat land and the river. Bandar took a jar of ash and put it in the storeroom with the label: *The Dead Eunuch.*

After the funeral, Somna went to sleep. She did not open her eyes for six months. When she did awaken, she was gaunt and weak. She asked to see the river and fell asleep, and dreamed her last dream of running.

The Stroller

When Bandar was an old man and labeled jars lined the storeroom from floor to ceiling, he built a stroller. Made of redwood, the stroller fit his dimensions perfectly: five-foot-nine-and-a-half and two-feet wide. He built a sun-top for the stroller and padded it with Somna's bright cloaks. Through the last eunuch left alive, he sent word to Mez to make him a white shift.

She sewed him one, fashioned after a baby's christening gown, and brought it to him in her alligator pumps and black dress. She, too, was old. The townspeople thought she wore black as an expression of mourning for the loss of James. Bandar knew she was sprouting into a Char Minar woman. He asked her age, and Mez told him she did not remember but she knew she was too old to bleed. It pleased him that she had returned to a childish state. He asked her if she remembered Somna running with him strapped to her front. He told her he had long ago deciphered the astrologer's riddle and realized that he, Bandar, would always be different. He had been carried on two in the morning, been driven on four in the afternoon, and now would be pushed on four at night. Showing Mez the stroller, he asked her if she would wheel him around. She said, yes, she would take him to a place, on land, facing sea, the place she had always thought of.

They left the house in the care of the lone eunuch and threw the key to the storeroom in the river. The last time the town saw them, Mez was pushing the stroller east, and Bandar looked out backward from under the sun-top, crying like the monkeys he was named for.

Sita and
Ms. Durber

Ms. Durber will not buy sensible shoes. She clicks to the coffeepot, breezing past faculty lounge titters and silences. Mr. Jershov, who will retire at the end of the year, calls her a prime filly. The art teacher, Mrs. Gould, retorts that Virginia Durber is not yet old enough to know how feet flatten and swell. "She'll change her style," Mrs. Gould says, "once she's taught on her puppies for twenty-five years."

Ms. Durber's thirty-four-year-old feet are beginning to spread. She is developing varicose veins. But she will not succumb. A pair of hearts mark the skyscraper boots she wears today. She totters around the kindergarten class-room, collecting drawings of cotton-ball trees, two-legged dogs. She praises the artistry of every child, believing that all of them are special and unique.

It is naptime. Ms. Durber hangs the student artwork. On a purple blanket the child, Sita, looks out at the classroom from under a low bridge of wooden chair legs. Two rows of blocks form a barricade in front of her blanket. She watches as Ms. Durber hangs her drawing: a penciled sketch of a cat stretching in a garden of tall hollyhocks and snapdragons, the fuzz on each bud luridly detailed and mirrored in the hairs on the inside of the cat's ears. There is a tiny, perfect beetle, wings raised, bowing a dandelion in the moment before flight.

The child comes to school lugging a black briefcase with a combination lock. Inside she keeps practice sketches and brown lunch bags filled with dead insects, specimens she examines at her desk with a jeweler's glass. She has been working on a grasshopper for weeks, its carcass brown and crispy. She sketches it, anatomically, on graph paper, each line corresponding to a numbered square. Ms. Durber hears Sita explain to Sonya, the chattiest girl in class, that she is attempting Dürer's *Konterfei* method. "It means 'making exactly like.' As in realism," she says. Sonya responds that she likes confetti, too.

Sita holds her pencil at the nub. To make dark lines, she stands on a chair and grasps the pencil with both hands.

Sita and Ms. Durber

Still, the lines are not dark enough. She goes over them with a stick of graphite. At recess, she dangles from a swing, letting the wind move her and watching the clouds with a detached superiority. When she notices Ms. Durber walking toward her, she drops from the rubber seat and hides under the slide, the tin chute buckling and thudding above her as the other children plunge down into a pile of woodchips.

For self-portraits, Sita uses a calligraphy brush and grey ink. In a stretched, unbroken stroke, she creates an outline of herself, leaving her body and face unfilled. Somehow these portraits do not appear blank or lacking; they are roomy, full of potential. Ms. Durber cannot figure out how this is achieved in one line. She and the sixth graders walk the kindergarten children to their buses. The teacher makes sure that Sita is in her group, and as she lifts the girl onto the first step of the bus, she is gratified to hear a tiny-voiced "Thank you." She watches Sita's bus pull away, the voice simmering inside her like an accomplishment.

When she learns Sita is a whiz with computers, Ms. Durber (who cannot stand the contraptions) staples together a construction-paper crown and pronounces Sita "Queen of the K-class Machines," during a mock coronation to which she wears her strappy sandals. She is pleased that Sita seems to like a boy who wets his pants constantly, and, loud with pride, announces his act. The girl reads aloud during Book-

Where the Long Grass Bends

Time, so fast and smoothly the other children are shy of volunteering. Ms. Durber encourages everyone to take turns. She tries to pull Sita onto her lap and is hurt when the child crouches among the computer tables.

Sometimes Ms. Durber finds charcoal portraits of herself in the trash. In the pictures, her face is expressionless. She is always depicted in action, writing on the blackboard, cleaning a child's face, bending at the water fountain. She rescues her likeness, brings the portraits home and puts them in a folder, certain that one day, the sketches will be valuable. All are signed with a microscopic "sp" in the lower left corner. Once in a while, Ms. Durber shows the pictures to the ninth- and tenth-grade teachers who make snide comments about her having time for her wardrobe because she has no essays to grade. Ms. Durber knows what they really think. That she has time and money because she has no children of her own.

Although her capabilities exceed the class, Sita shows no desire to leave or move faster. The other children shun her. They struggle to keep letters inside dotted training lines, pronouncing silent *k*'s and *p*'s, fisting their crayons and pounding out rough interpretations of their families and pets. They exclude Sita from their play as if she is stupid and uncomprehending of what it is to be a kindergartner. When she presents two girls with a sketch of

Sita and Ms. Durber

an elaborately furnished dollhouse they say, "You talk like a grown-up!" and turn away. Ms. Durber watches Sita's face contort, but the child does not cry. She leaves her sketch on top of a box of markers and walks away, blushing. For the remainder of the day she does not speak and toils over her drawings, her face and tense fingers vaguely mutinous.

During the third month of school, Sita becomes malicious. Ms. Durber does not scold her, although she knows she should. She watches with a reckless, scientific interest as Sita builds architecturally sound models of The Forbidden City, then knocks over the hovels and shacks of her classmates. When the children flub words during Book-Time, she ignores Sita's snickers. The girl sings the alphabet backward, tripping up those just learning their letters. Ms. Durber says mildly, "Don't, Sita, give them a chance." She watches as the child, wretched and industrious, hauls a lump of raw clay from her briefcase and molds it into an army of identical statuettes with the pale, blind look of miners. Ms. Durber asks why all the statues look alike. Sita does not answer.

"I'm only trying to help," Ms. Durber says. "Don't you want to be helped?" Sita pushes her hair out of her face and continues to sculpt.

Ms. Durber feels the child is disturbed, unhealthily

sequestered. She goes to the main office and borrows Sita's file, learning that her parents own the restaurant on the south side of Front Street, and that she attends the school on scholarship. Along with the application for aid, her mother sent one of the child's drawings: a man with dreadlocks and sinewy arms running in the rain, holding a newspaper open to the business section (the Dow is up) over his head. The picture makes Ms. Durber feel soggy. On the back, the acceptance committee had written: *motor skills not puerile* followed by a streak of exclamation points, and *check date of birth* amid a flock of question marks.

Hoping to encourage, Ms. Durber buys Sita a small notebook with a purple silk cover and red spine. The pages feel like linen and are creamy white. She slips it to Sita at recess, saying, "Don't tell the others," surprised when the child takes out a pencil and immediately begins to draw. On the first page, she sketches Ms. Durber's face with a background of animal-style, interlocking lines and vines.

"It's lovely," Ms. Durber says, and her eyes water with pleasure, "Very van Gogh, but richer and more sublime." The strangeness of saying *van Gogh* and *sublime* to a five-year-old, without explanation, strikes her, and she looks guiltily away so Sita will not see her discomfort. The child devotes the next page of the notebook to a watercolor of a grasshopper in a green, wind-driven world of weeds that spring and flow.

Mrs. Parthivendra hugs Sita, takes the briefcase, and gives the child what looks like an orange milkshake. Sita leans against her mother's leg. The woman wears a full, pleated silk skirt, a long-sleeved silk blouse, and very white sneakers. "What an interesting outfit," Ms. Durber exclaims.

Mrs. Parthivendra arches an eyebrow. "I've come from the restaurant," she says, and the teacher nods.

"It's so good to meet the mother of this remarkable child. Sita is a pleasure to have in class. Though, I have noticed that what with her... abilities, she seems, well, somewhat... isolated."

The girl's mother looks around the classroom and at Sita slurping noisily on her drink. "She's different," she says.

"But she *is* a child. I think she needs to have more fun. She works extremely hard."

Mrs. Parthivendra smoothes Sita's hair, and says something to her that Ms. Durber does not understand. To the teacher she says: "Sita plays the cello; we go to museums, the opera, places like that. That's how she has fun. We are not ignorant people. In Malaysia, I was a surgeon, and her father, a well-known architect."

"I didn't mean to imply…it's just…she could do more ordinary…," Ms. Durber sighs and falls silent as Mrs. Parthivendra hikes up her sleeves. There is a spot of flour near her elbow and her forearms are lean and strong. The teacher feels awed by her tart, Britishlike accent.

"If you really think, Ms. Durber, that Sita needs to be more ordinary, *you* may help her."

"It would be my pleasure, but—"

"I'm sorry. We must go." The teacher hears injury in Mrs. Parthivendra's tone. The woman takes Sita's hand, and the child sucks at her drink. Both walk with the same purposeful gait. They shut the door quietly behind them.

"Haughty witch," Ms. Durber says, out loud, as she refills the stapler.

Ms. Durber keeps a close watch over Sita, who unexpectedly abandons her briefcase in a Dumpster and comes to school with her insects and jeweler's glass in a fanny pack. The child sits in class, slack and bored. She is only eager during free-draw when she sketches her own left hand, over and over again. Each picture is increasingly realistic with added stratums of tendon, derma, follicles. The supremacy has dropped from her gaze and been replaced with a look of wary interest. The children are more accepting of her, too. Ms. Durber is glad to have talked with

Sita and Ms. Durber

Mrs. Parthivendra. She laughs as the pant-wetting boy plays with a yo-yo and Sita sits next to him trying to touch the toy as it unwinds and chirping in surprise as the boy spools it up. In the halls, Sita holds Ms. Duber's wrist and sometimes allows herself to be embraced. During recess, she sits under a tree and pages through Ms. Durber's art history books from college. Sometimes she looks through a piece of white paper, punctuated by a small hole. This particular game intrigues Ms. Durber. She follows Sita outside and asks what she is doing.

The child holds the page to her eye, looking through the hole at the bark of a tree. Without lowering the paper she says: "Local color. Brown in bright light is a different color than brown next to red or brown in shadow. Color changes when isolated." She moves away from the teacher, toward some dark green pachysandra.

Ms. Durber is ecstatic. She takes the punctured paper from the trash where Sita tosses it, and brings it home. She adds it to the folder filled with portraits. She can hear herself telling the story of Sita and "local color" to interviewers from *Biography*, or *Bravo*, or *Lifetime*. She decides that on Saturday, she will take the child to the circus for some ordinary fun (if the mother approves) and bring along her own ten-year-old nephew.

• • •

Sita looks smaller out of uniform, wearing a red coat over a black dress with a lace pinafore and festive red shoes. She waits patiently outside the driver's side of the car. Ms. Durber rolls down the window, "Yes, Sita? Why don't you get in the backseat?"

The child holds a square, wrapped offering above her head, and through the window Ms. Durber takes it. As Sita sits, Ms. Durber speaks sharply to her nephew: "Nelson, this is my student, Sita. Help her with her seat belt, please." The boy, in jeans and a sweatshirt, a ski jacket balled under his feet, leans over the girl and fastens her belt.

"Pretty dressed up for the circus, aren't you?" he asks.

Unwrapping the present, Ms. Durber finds a box of Darjeeling tea and a gift certificate to the restaurant on Front Street. She says, "Thank you, Sita. How thoughtful of your parents." The child looks at Nelson's sneakers. Built-in red lights flash from the heels.

At the circus, Ms. Durber buys Nelson and Sita what look like plastic whisks growing out of flashlights. When a button is depressed, the plastic strands light up, blue and white. Sita shakes the whisk making small noises of admiration and shock. Her noises increase when a clown, with a glowing orb clenched between his teeth, seats them in a dark stadium lit with long spotlights that wheel around the crowd. Quickly, Sita sketches the clown in her notebook.

Sita and Ms. Durber

A family of four takes up the row behind Ms. Durber, Nelson, and Sita. A girl, about the same age as Sita, sits directly behind her. The girl has on a pink jogging suit and her blonde hair shines with a green, chlorinated tint. She snorts like a pig, bounces, rolls her eyes dramatically when her mother asks her to stop, empties a container of Jujubes on the floor, and makes her little brother pick them up. Sita cranes around in her seat and watches the girl. "Ignore her," Ms. Durber says. "She's trying to get attention."

Nelson asks to be excused. "I hafta pee," he says, and Sita stares at him.

Under the lights, a parade of white horses prance, plumed with lime green feathers and satin saddles. Sita does a sketch of the elephants' baggy knees. A chimpanzee tiptoes across a wire, and a tamer in striped jodhpurs whirls in and out of a flaming hoop. The crowd hollers appreciation. The girl behind Sita stands on her chair and pumps her fists above her head shouting "Yes Yes Yes," the spotlight spins and whirls, the wild repetitive music crescendoes, and the stage goes black. Moments later, an oval light centers in the middle of the circus-ring and lights up a bearded magician in a cape. The girl behind Sita bawls out "Holy Good God Shit!" and cries in piggish snorts when her mother slaps her.

Ms. Durber turns to Sita. The child looks cold,

hunched inside her jacket. Her notebook lies open to a blank page. The stadium floods with a low light, and four motorcycles race in a huge, rodent-exercise wheel. Sita whimpers and squeezes her eyes shut. Ms. Durber says: "It's just for show. Don't worry," and tries to hug the child. She feels Sita's forehead. It is clammy.

Nelson returns from the bathroom with two hot dogs for himself and Sita. She sniffs hers, then slyly watches Nelson eat. "You usually have it with mustard," he tells her, "but they were out of it." With one hand Sita pushes the hot dog into her mouth, with the other she sketches a small picture of a frankfurter and under it, in parentheses, writes *(the hot dog is usually eaten with mustard)*. She is calmer now that the motorcycles have left the stage and been replaced with jugglers and a circle of flames. On the next page of her notebook, she sketches a full-body portrait of Nelson. At the bottom of the page, she writes: *I hafta pee*. She shows it to the boy, who laughs: "Hey, that's really good."

When a midget appears on a saddled ostrich, Sita sits up attentively and asks Ms. Durber, "Is that a child?" She seems horrified to learn that the man is a dwarf and whispers, "I read about one in 'The Potato Elf.'"

Pulling the child onto her lap, the teacher says, "Just have fun. Don't think about anything." She is thankful when Sita sags against her.

Sita and Ms. Durber

But then two clowns appear. The music and lights speed up, and Sita begins to whimper. Slipping from Ms. Durber's grasp, she turns around in her seat. The girl with the green-blonde hair sleeps with her thumb in her mouth, curled in a ball around her little brother. Sita stands on her chair and screams in short, sharp blasts.

Entrusting her purse to Nelson, Ms. Durber carries Sita from the stadium. The child stops screaming and puts her thumb in her mouth, but Ms. Durber pulls it out and dries it with a tissue. "Stop that," she chides. "You'll ruin your teeth."

In the car, Sita flings her head back in a posture of snoring, loud piglike rumblings emitting from her throat. As soon as Ms. Durber pulls up in front of the child's house, Sita grabs her light-whisk from Nelson and runs from the car, leaving the door open. Nelson leans over and slams it shut. "She's loony," he says to his aunt, "and she left her notebook. We didn't even get to see the Flying Ciancio Brothers."

Ms. Durber receives a call from Mrs. Parthivendra. The woman is distraught; she says Sita refuses to play the cello or read. At dinner, she threw her food on the floor and demanded a hot dog. "We are vegetarian," Mrs. Parthivendra says, bewildered.

"It's just a phase," Ms. Durber replies, nervously. "She's trying new things. I'm sure she'll get tired of it soon."

The teacher cools the guilty feeling in her stomach with a gin and tonic. Flipping through Sita's notebook, she decides the clown with the orb in his mouth is frightening. She looks through the portraits in her folder. There is something dark and threatening in Sita's shadow depictions, the way she draws the lines around Ms. Durber's mouth. The teacher looks at the portraits and doesn't quite recognize herself. The penciled woman seems frenetic, desperate, like she is rushing toward something, but with a face completely devoid of motion.

When she sees Sita back at school, Ms. Durber recognizes the small, solemn child with relief. Through lunch and recess, Sita pages through the dictionary and refuses Ms. Durber's hand in the hall. She builds her fort of chairs and blocks, staring suspiciously at the other children while they nap. Ms. Durber feels exonerated and tries to return the girl's notebook, but Sita runs and crouches beneath a computer table. During free-draw, she shields her picture with her body when Ms. Durber tries to take a peek.

At the end of the day, Ms. Durber sits in the empty classroom and writes a thank-you note to Sita's parents for the tea and gift certificate. She rearranges the apples and potted silk plants on her desk and rummages through the garbage for Sita's work from free-draw—an elegant sketch of a hunched midget with a red plastic nose, sitting on a grinning clown's lap.

Five
Objects
in
Queens

White Nova. Circa 1979. Astoria, Queens.

They used the backseat for misdemeanors. The eldest, Rita, smoked cigarettes there and hid lipstick under the floor mat. Rita's little sister, Priyanka, rolled up the windows, stretched out on the cushy, red leather (smelling of rotten French fries and incense), and attempted to sing like Aretha Franklin. Their grandmother, Dado, surreptitiously chucked her insulin in the neighbor's trashcan and hunkered there to eat half a Ring Ding and Ayurvedic tablets.

It was their cousin Bablu's car. After a bout of speeding tickets, his license was suspended, and he parked the Nova in front of their building beneath the dogwood tree. He left the keys so they could move the car for street cleaning and he came by on Sundays to scrub off the white flowers that littered the hood.

The first time Dado sat in the backseat of the Nova, she huffed: "Marutis are nicer." She would not sit in front, saying it was too close to "evil *asura* face," and pointing to the bulging headlights. She had come from Bombay, for June and July, to look after her granddaughters. Her son, Kumar, and his wife, Mary, were visiting relatives in Bangalore. They had left the rules of the household on the refrigerator, under a Yosemite Sam magnet.

> *Number 1: No Driving*
> *Number 2: No Sweets.*

All were in agreement that numbers three through twelve were irrelevant. Since the rules did not specify, the girls ate no sweets, and Dado did not drive. Rita (she had her learner's permit) took her sister for spins around the neighborhood, but only after Priyanka swore, crossing her heart, not to sing. They drove by their father's store, Rita smoking like a demon in lipstick, and checked that Bablu, the boss till August, had remembered to turn off the lights. Kumar was particular about his electricity bills.

During that thick, hot summer, Priyanka's senses

deceived her into hearing the clang of goat bells in Kalyan Camp (their father had told them stories of his childhood there). She tried to interest Rita in playing "Refugee" and tied a bell around her own neck, mewling like a starving cat. Her sister was bored by the game and sat on Priyanka until she agreed to play gin rummy instead.

They lived on the first floor—no stairs to lug the groceries up, but the slamming of the building door percussed their days. The noise did not bother Dado; she was partially deaf. When she watched television, the Karyatises, who lived next door, banged on their shared wall and cursed in Greek. Dado turned the volume up, and lectured the girls on Jimmy Carter and the oil embargo. "No more auto," she said, wagging her finger at them. "Take the subway like good citizen." The sisters wagged their fingers back, saying, "OK. No more sweets," at which time Dado lost her ability to understand English.

In between singing lullabies to herself, Dado talked to the television. "Iran," she said to it. "What do you know of Iran?" There was a Persian family on the news whose house in Deer Park had been looted. "See—they look like us," she said. She instructed the girls to yell "*Jhule, Jhulelal*," if any *kafirs* came to the apartment. Then she would know to dial 911, also magneted to the fridge. "If bad people enter, you must kick and bite," she said, baring her teeth. Priyanka nodded, "Don't worry, we will." She thought of her father's stories of the blood and fire of his last days in Sindh.

The girls did not tell their parents (who called once a week) when they found the empty urine container Dado was supposed to fill. Instead, they made iced tea in the gallon jug and brought it outside to drink on the stoop. When the Good Humor man came by, Dado sailed out in her white sari and ate half an Italian ice. She saved the wooden paddle and used it to stir her before-bed tea. Their parents had said to never let Dado take sugar, even in her tea, but when the girls reminded her of that, she moaned: "I have lost my Sindhri. One kilo of flour, that is all they gave us. At least I will be happy with the KitKat in my *pate*."

The only concession she would make was to eat half of each sweet. She cooked massive dinners, every night a new recipe, and was forever complaining about the dullness of American produce. She felt sorry for supermarket eggplants and tomatoes and said, meaningfully raising her eyebrows at Rita: "*Bharat me, subjiyan khush hai*."

"What about vegetables?" Priyanka asked.

"In India, vegetables are happy," Rita translated.

One Thursday, after a long puja for Virol Bhagwan, it

was too hot for words. The Manhattan skyline, looking oily, pierced the haze. Everyone sat out on their stoops; the R train snaked and rattled under the sidewalk. Some Greek kids tried to open a fire hydrant at the end of the block. Mr. Woo, the grandfather in 2A, refereed a game of dominoes. Rita was wearing a new pink sundress. It had a childish, elastic bodice crimped with crisscrosses of white thread and straps that tied into bows at the tops of her shoulders. "The Nova has A/C," she said craftily, twirling an imaginary mustache, "we could go for a *chakkar* to cool down."

"Genius," Priyanka responded. She asked if she could borrow the new dress, but Rita, brandishing the privilege of age, said no.

Dado did not feel well. Purple bruises covered her hands, and she walked unsteadily as though she could not feel her feet. The girls made mashed potatoes and wrapped a shawl around their grandmother. They put her in their mother's moccasins (she looked like she was standing in gondolas), slipped an Ayurvedic tablet under her tongue, and sat her in the backseat of the Nova. Driving up and down the streets, the girls sucked in their cheeks and made fish faces at each other. They blasted the air-conditioning and squeezed the mashed potatoes from sandwich bags into their mouths. Dado perked up, sang songs of Kishinchand

Bewas, her feet propped on the window she insisted upon opening, her thin, white braid whipping in the wind.

At the north end of Astoria, they saw a movie theatre. The sign around the Marquis, lit by naked yellow bulbs, advertised a FREEZING INTERIOR. A girl with her name scrawled across her neck in diamonds sold them tickets to the longest movie. Dado ate half a box of Goobers. On the way home, in the backseat, she fell asleep. She said it was her best nap since she was a girl in her mother's arms.

"Call Mary," she told her granddaughters as they tucked her into bed. "Call your mother and say hello."

Gardening Gloves. Circa 1980. Astoria, Queens.

The gloves were green, the palms lined with rubber nodules that looked, to Kumar, like taste buds. Mary said they were good for grip.

A narrow dirt plot stretched behind the building. The other tenants had no interest in gardening, and the landlord told Mary she could harvest the yard—an eighth of an acre more wondrous to her than the Botanical Gardens. She planted Emperor tulips, a rhododendron bush with waxen leaves and lavender blooms. Her roses (Kumar named them after Mughal emperors: Akbar,

Jahangir, Shah Jahan, the thorniest one: Aurangzeb) were robust, the soil around their roots pampered with special treatments of ground eggshells and diced banana peels.

"Roses don't die; they turn into something else," Mary liked to say as she arranged the yellow, red, and white petals on plates. Inside the apartment, cups and glasses burst with roses, some tight to the bud or frosted and festooned, some cut long and stripped of their serrated greens. The small tea roses Mary decapitated and floated with candles in bowls of water. Priyanka's and Rita's drawers overflowed with potpourri, and Mary bottled rose water, left it stoppered by the bathtub, so Kumar could spill some in while he soaked. At the end of the season, she made rose-hip tea. Rita said it tasted greasy, but the idea of drinking roses delighted Priyanka and she had cup after cup.

Mary spoiled her flora. She made coffee just for the zinnias and managed to contain the bamboo along the back fence in a neat, rectangular grove. She liked the way it creaked when the wind blew. A couple of rows into the bamboo, she tucked a small statue of the Virgin Mary and one of Shirdi Sai Baba. Despite Kumar's pleading, she refused to raise anything functional—no herbs or vegetables, nothing edible. She grew only beautiful, frivolous things.

Kumar could not be in the garden if she was

transplanting. The sound of roots being ripped, the separation of clustered flowers, upset him. He said it sounded like loss, like eviction: "It's not natural to leave roots behind."

"That's why flowers put out so many, so some will survive. Like the Irish and children." Mary rinsed her gloves at the garden hose and wrung them out. "If you and my grandmother hadn't uprooted, we would have no Priyanka, no Rita."

"True, true," Kumar said. Still, when Mary transplanted, he stayed inside.

Every summer, Mary trained jasmine to climb a six-foot trellis. When the delicate flowers bloomed, Kumar took his plastic folding chair and sat, saying the smell of *mogra* reminded him of Sikanderabad. No one was allowed to talk to him for at least an hour while he closed his eyes and wandered around his memory.

Once, the four of them drove to the Rockaways on what Kumar called "The Great Seaweed March." They piled out of the car (Mary in her green gloves, striding over the sand), the ocean rolling and sucking at their feet, each carrying a black trash bag that ballooned in the wind. They filled the bags with seaweed they pulled from the water or found on shore, hulking masses of it, covered with pods that Rita snapped all the way home.

Five Objects in Queens

After poking holes in the trash bags and draining the salt water, the seaweed was dumped over the germinating sections of Mary's garden. "We Irish take the sea seriously," she said to the girls, "and use all it offers. It's an old Galway trick my mother taught me." It was Rita's and Priyanka's job to rinse the seaweed until the tang of salt faded. They taste-tested, dabbing their tongues on the slick leaves. Until the seaweed dried out, the backyard smelled like a beach.

At the end of the bamboo grove was Mary's prized Japanese maple. The girls had dug the hole for it while their mother was on bedrest after her lumpectomy. She sat in Kumar's lawn chair, watching as they worked. Rita had been sullen; she wanted to go shopping with friends. Priyanka told her to stop sulking, and Mary said she could mold a better face out of hot shit. Then Kumar arrived back from a nursery in Hicksville. He waddled into the yard, carrying a dwarf Japanese maple, its roots bound in sacking and twine. He lowered the huge bulb into the hole, and he and Mary took seven steps around the tree, hand in hand, to tamp down the soil.

Every fall, Mary waited with excitement until the maple leaves curled and drifted from the tree. Raking was therapeutic and brought her closer to the girls, like the day Priyanka came home from school, quiet. Someone had said she looked funny. Mary took her out in the garden and they raked and bagged the dark, nearly black, maple leaves, scattered in a circle around the slender trunk of the tree. She told Priyanka to never be concerned with what other people said. She and Rita were Indian and Irish, a particular kind of American, and if somebody didn't like it, well, they could stuff it or come and speak to her about it.

She always seemed fiercer in the garden. She defended the lilies from aphids with mail-order ladybugs—a red-winged army delivered in plastic cells. Her war on slugs was well-plotted and tied to her mood. Whenever Priyanka and Rita sassed her, Mary said: "Gardenias don't talk back," and stalked off with a canister of salt. They watched her from the window, putting on her green gloves, kicking off her moccasins, opening the small tin chute on the Morton's container. She poured salt over the slugs till a pall of white crystals covered them. With satisfaction, she watched them ooze and hummed "Danny Boy."

The girls took to calling their mother Garden Moo. They spoke in a secret, teenage language that infuriated Kumar and amused Mary. If Rita was feeling bold, she would moo at her mother, but it was an unsatisfying game because Mary either told her to grow up or mooed back.

At times, Mary stood still in the garden, stroking the velvety geranium leaves, listening to the bamboo creak, the subway underfoot. She thought of Kumar and how, when the girls were young and his store still a dream, she would run her green, gloved hands over his face. He said her fingers felt like ten licking tongues. They had lived in a one-bedroom apartment then, and stayed up late, talking about the future in whispers. Priyanka and Rita shared a bed, the pull-out couch. They slept on their stomachs, their heads turned to face each other, their small biceps touching.

Brown Ceramic Plate. Circa 1984. Astoria, Queens.

The summer before Rita's last year at college, Kumar set aside a plate for himself. The plate was brown. It was deep, bowllike, and at its center bloomed a pink lotus. He liked the plate because he could use it for solid and liquidy meals. With permanent marker, he drew a "K" on the bottom, and told the women they were not to touch it.

He knew of no other man who lived with three females, jabbering and drifting away from him, bickering and screaming at each other. And just as Kumar became enraged enough to join in, they all turned on him for trying to involve himself in their affairs. Even the cat was a girl. In retaliation, Kumar had his plate. He made up titles for his unwritten autobiography. His wallet was stuffed with lists: "Kumar's Pet Peeves," "Movies Kumar Needs To

Rent," "People Kumar Should Throttle." He was tired of selling things, of figuring out his customers and pitching what they wanted to hear. He bought Bablu's Nova and kept up the Sunday buffings.

How the women howled when they found only their names on a list entitled, "Know-It-Alls Kumar Is Familiar With." It was Mary who discovered the list when she borrowed a book from his nightstand. She called to her daughters, who had agreed not to speak to her (Moo the Maniac) after she yelled at them for overwatering the lilacs. When Mary showed them the list, the girls forgave her instantly. They all collapsed on the sofa and laughed, slapping their hands against their knees and clutching each other. Kumar found them laughing when he came home, and between the three of them setting each other off, they finally managed to make him understand what was so funny. The only response he could think of—"Well, this is what I mean!"—made them laugh even harder.

In July, Kumar got a dog from the pound, a St. Bernard mutt who came with a keg attached to his collar. The dog was supposed to be Kumar's ally (he named him Pal), but Pal chose Rita as his love (she renamed him Bernie, short for Bernadette). Mary would not let Bernie in the garden because he pissed on the roses. Priyanka, too, did not like the dog. When she walked him, he allowed her to lead till the apartment building was out of sight, then sat down. No matter how Priyanka pulled, the dog stayed firm, panting and looking off behind her (her face pinked with exertion, eyes swilling with tears), and when Bernie decided he wanted to go back home, he dragged Priyanka.

If Rita walked the dog, he waited till they reached the neighborhood park before seating himself. She readily agreed and sat next to him. Observing the mallards and geese, they rested, and anyone watching them would think they decided together and simultaneously when to go home. Rita filled the dog's keg with Kool-Aid, Priyanka's favorite drink, convinced her sister would always need more rescuing than herself.

At the end of the summer, Mary went into the hospital for a round of chemo and a CT scan. Another lump had been found in her right breast. She said she didn't want people mooning around her, making a fuss. She forced Rita to take her food shopping immediately after the procedures.

They had a good time together until they got to the check-out counter, where Mary held up the line fumbling around in her wallet for exact change. Irritated, Rita left her mother and wandered out to the gumball machines. One machine held fluorescent green Buddhas, each one twenty-five cents. Rita was suddenly struck by a childish desire to buy two. One for Priyanka and one for Kumar, she decided. Since she had only one quarter, she waited till her mother came out of the store, wheeling the groceries through the first set of automatic doors. "What are you doing, Reetu?" Mary asked.

"I want to buy Yanka and Dad a Buddha, but I only have one quarter." Rita answered her mother peevishly. She was afraid Mary would say she was too old to buy toys from gumball machines.

Mary took her hands from the shopping cart and balled them into fists. "Pick one," she singsonged, as the automatic doors shut with a squeal behind her. Rita touched her left hand to Mary's left fist and laughed with surprise when her mother opened the hand to reveal a quarter. She laughed again as Mary opened her other fist, and Rita saw a quarter shining in that palm, too. "Take them both. Buddhas on me," Mary said.

"I don't know how she did, it, Yanka," Rita told her sister that evening. They both agreed, in honor of their mother's trick, to change her name to Magical Moo.

The next morning, Kumar awoke in a state. He pounded on the girls' door, "Priyanka? Rita? Get up and get out here. I know you used my plate. You better bloody well show me where you hid it."

Rita pretended to be asleep. Priyanka roused herself and went to the kitchen. "What's the matter, Daddy?"

Five Objects in Queens

"My plate," he shouted, "where did you hide it?"

"I'll help you look," Priyanka soothed. "Don't wake up Moo. She was sick last night. I heard you guys."

Kumar took everything out of the cupboards and piled it all on the kitchen floor: mugs, glasses, plates, tiffins, *atto*, spaghetti, bags of rice, boxes of raisins and figs. He flounced around the kitchen, not even noticing when Rita joined her sister in search of the missing plate. The girls emptied the pantry, too, and stacked its contents in the hall and living room. They ignored Kumar and chatted with each other, "Oh my gawd, this pot is so seventies." "When you get married, you should ask for these knives."

For two hours, they searched the kitchen, then moved into the hall and living room. The girls emptied everything and Kumar moved behind them, calmly reorganizing and restocking shelves. He told them a few stories they had never heard before about living in Bombay and sneaking into American movies, about a man who sold *sitapul* and walked around with a parrot on his shoulder.

Close to nine o'clock, Mary woke and heard them. She trundled out of the bedroom in her nightgown and slippers and stared in disbelief at Kumar and the girls standing in the kitchen surrounded by empty cabinets, heaps of food, china. She started to bend and pick up a box of cereal, but Priyanka grabbed her shoulders. She looked into her mother's face, saw the small lines and wrinkles around her eyes. She pulled Mary's hands to her own cheeks and laughed as her mother said, "Yanka, what *are* you doing?"

Priyanka shouted, "Run, Magical, Run!"

Mary looked at her laughing daughters and over at Kumar standing with a can of creamed corn in his hand. She turned and fled, out the door of the apartment, then the door of the building, her nightgown twisting around her legs.

When she came home, it was lunchtime. She said she felt better, not so weak or nauseated. Kumar found his plate in the dishwasher. He took it out and wiped the central lotus lovingly. "Girls," he called, "it was me, not you."

Snorkel with Blue Rim and Dolphin Insignia. Circa 1991. Astoria, Queens.

Mary and Kumar had the apartment to themselves. Rita lived in Brooklyn with a woman named Grace, their one-year-old adopted daughter, and Bernadette the St. Bernard. Priyanka and her Jamaican husband (his great-great-grandfather had been Indian, an indentured servant on a sugar plantation) lived in Manhattan. Every Saturday, the three families met in Astoria. Most weekends, the girls stayed Sunday, too, helping their mother in the garden, sitting on the stoop with their father. A lump had been found in Mary's back.

Kumar no longer slept through the night. When he did sleep, he dreamed in Sindhi, and cried out for his dog George who had died forty-five years ago in Kalyan. Mary thought he needed more exercise, that the effort would help him rest. She signed him up for swimming lessons at the YMCA (even though Dado had always said "Indians don't swim"). It was hard for Kumar not to thrash and sink, his arms slashing hatefully at the blue water. Swimming was not relaxing as Mary had promised it would be. The instructor recommended he buy a snorkel, to help with buoyancy and learning his strokes.

The first time he took his snorkel to the pool, Mary went with him. She brought her own snorkel so he would not feel foolish being the only one at the Y dressed for the deep. Self-conscious of her scars, she wore a T-shirt over her bathing suit. Kumar wore one too, to keep her company.

The roof that covered the indoor pool was made of glass. Mary left her mask on the edge of the pool, did a lap of backstroke, and watched the sky going by. In the shallow end, she showed Kumar how to spit on the lens, then rinse it, how to honk into the snorkel and purge it of water, how to fit the mouthpiece between his teeth. They practiced breathing above water first. Kumar felt silly, too

143

old to be learning how to swim, too old to be wearing a
snorkel in a pool.

He adjusted his mask and slipped underwater alone,
Mary standing by to jerk him to safety if necessary. He could
see surprisingly well; it was like wearing his reading glasses.
There were Mary's legs, white and shimmering. He saw the
blue lane-dividers bobbing to his left and a child in a yellow
bathing suit kicking by. It was peaceful underwater, just the
sound of his lungs filling and expelling air, the sun warm on
his back. He felt gilled, womblike, as though his body was
remembering an old machinery. There seemed to be a layer
of quiet between himself and the rest of the world. Only
Mary, her legs and hands reassuringly close, was real. Kumar
put his feet down on the bottom of the pool and lifted his
head. The water rushed off the mask and he spit out the
mouthpiece: "S'wonderful!" he said. Mary smiled and put
on her mask.

They floated face-down, together, in the shallows.
Kumar breathed evenly and deeply, hearing the whoosh of
air, the pressure and slur of water in his ears. An old
woman went by fast in the far lane and the water around
him lifted and lurched. Mary's hair wafted about her face
like a disobedient spider plant. Her skin looked rubbery.
She reached out and took Kumar's hand. Behind the mask
and plastic seal, her eyes were magnified, her cheeks

squashed and striated. She made a circle with her thumb and index finger and gave Kumar an OK sign. He nodded. Looking down, Kumar saw his feet. They looked strangely flat. He pointed to them and scrunched up his face. Mary laughed. The sound was high-pitched. It burbled and hovered in the water.

They stayed like that, breathing, floating. Kumar watched rings of golden light twining on the bottom of the pool. He saw a Band-Aid drifting down there, and long strands of brown hair.

Cuticle Scissors. Circa 1994. Astoria, Queens.

Kumar sold half of the shop to Bablu and worked only three days a week. To keep occupied, he swam every morning and took an evening photography class at the Arts Center.

For his final project, he had planned to shoot Mary's flowers—the perennials—any that came up this first spring without her. But he found himself drawn to the items inside the apartment. It was the title of the assignment that struck him: *still life*. In these things, their life, Mary was still there. Everything he looked at represented an epic, an era. A pillow reminded him of Rita with the chicken pox; a spoon gave him Mary, pregnant, eating strawberry ice cream. The record player was Priyanka weeping to Sam Cooke's voice. He took a photograph of the dimmer switch and saw Dado's face the first time she slid it, and the kitchen lighting up like a morning in fast-forward.

He looked at the objects in the house, wondering what they had meant to Mary, not certain that he knew. It was what he missed most—talking to her, how she always surprised him. She would say something he hadn't expected, enjoy something he thought she would dislike. Thirty-two years: they had used these things together.

Passing a mirror, he realized he needed a haircut. Mary had always buzzed the back of his neck with electric clippers and called the barber to make his appointments. He decided to slick his hair with water. His daughters would worry if they saw him looking unkempt; they were due soon for dinner. He walked to the bathroom and opened the vanity drawer, searching for his comb.

There were Mary's cuticle scissors.

About fifteen years ago, when the girls were still in high school, Mary had baked a cherry pie. They finished the pie in one sitting, had it after dinner with Mysore coffee. While they were slumped in their chairs, fat, digesting, Dado called from Bombay to append a recipe. Her voice was crackling and distant; the girls held the telephone receiver between them: "Put two more tomaters in the

146

vangar to make it saucy, how Mary likes. I hope you have not told anybody the secret of pickling in water? Good girls. Put Daddy on. I am sick of English."

While Kumar talked to his mother, Mary left the table. She returned with a pair of cuticle scissors, ducked the phone cord, and tilted Kumar's head back. "Now hold still, this will just take a second," she said, her face puckered with concern as she trimmed the reckless tufts of his eyebrows.

Kumar pressed his hands against his damp hair. He heard the front door open, and the cat running for the safety of the bed.

"Daddy?" Priyanka and Rita called out in unison.

"Yes, yes, I'm here," he shouted back.

Bing-Chen

"It's too long," his mother said. "You look like a crazy bird."

His hair, brown, lank, was tufting around his ears.

"My girl's in Chinatown. Gives a good cut. Pretty, too. You could get me a newspaper; there was a flood near Guilin."

"It's fine," he said.

"Sticking up all over. Like a bird."

"Let's talk about something else."

"So much grey—you're starting to look like me."

"I'll go, I'll go, I'll get a haircut. What's the name of the paper?"

She twirled her brush, ground the ink.

"Just use a pen."

"David. You can wait a few minutes."

He watched her hands, the knuckles fat and crippled. She put the brush to paper, her strokes lean; the two black characters shiny.

"Show it to the vendor," she said. "You won't even have to open your mouth."

David took the subway to Grand Street, his mother's directions and the name of the newspaper in his pocket. A heat welled from the sidewalk. He eased through the crowds to a produce stall selling cabbages, spiny leechees, winter melon. His mouth watered when he saw the pomegranates.

To avoid a huddle of tourists, he walked in the street. He passed stalls crammed with wind chimes, wicker birdcages, calculators, dolls with motorized, wagging heads, black cloth shoes with tin buckles, then consulted his mother's directions. *Get off subway. Go south and east. Second right. Chicken store on corner.*

There, plucked and hanging in the window. Four of them, with talons, and glazed, blue eyes. Chickens had dangerous feet. On the plate, in pieces, they seemed harmless. He turned right.

It was an alley, not a street, and it smelled of fish.

Bing-Chen

Laundry flapped from the fire escapes. A woman in a white shirt leaned from a window, smoking a cigarette.

He could still buy the newspaper and go home.

But it was hot. His hair felt sticky. He might as well get it cut.

The door swung open, inward. His mother's girl. She was Chinese, of course. With dyed-blonde hair and square, pink-painted nails. She said, "Ni hao ma."

David shook his head.

She laughed. "OK. Come in," and pulled him through the door.

"You're third. I have two other customers. Prom day."

She led him from a dark foyer to a wide, square room. On a couch was a woman filing her nails. David sat down. The nail file rasped, rasped.

There was only one counter, one mirror, one chair. Pictures of cats and Tom Cruise were taped in neat rows around the mirror. The girl stood in front of it, scissors in hand, and snipped at the ends of her blonde hair. She wore a pink tennis dress and white high heels. There were Band-Aids across the backs of her ankles.

The woman rose from the couch and disappeared through a red-beaded partition. She left the nail file.

153

"Bye, Ma." The girl raked her fingers through her hair, and peered at her roots in the mirror.

"You Chinese, Mister?"

"Half," he said.

There was a knock at the door. The girl dunked the scissors in a container filled with Windex-colored fluid and black combs.

"Who's Chinese? Ma or Da?"

"My mother," David said. "My father was American. German."

The girl laughed, "My mother washes hair, my father works at bank," and walked with light taps to the door.

A brunette and a red-haired girl stood glowing in the stairwell light. Both girls held transparent, plastic bags. The brunette went through the red beads for a hair-washing. She had curly hair, tight, thick curls, hair that grew out, not down. Her body curved with the softness of porn stars, a good shape over nice bones. As the red beads clicked around her, she lifted her shoulders and cringed.

The other girl was hard-faced and deeply tanned. She moved the nail file and sat down on the couch with David. "So, Ming," she said, "do you want to hear about my dress?"

"OK, sure."

"I got it at Bloomie's. It's black organdy with a trim of

pearls. Strapless. My mother says it looks perfect with my red hair."

"Nice," Ming said, but her lips stuck to her teeth, dry and false. The girl waved her mother's check between her fingers, its amount line blank. When Ming did not walk over to collect it, the girl dropped it on the floor next to the couch.

To David she said, "Me and Marcy come to Chinatown just for Ming. My mom discovered her last year. Our cleaning lady comes here, too. She's so cheap, it's scary. Ming, I mean, not our maid."

What a voice. Husky, like she'd been smoking twenty years longer than she'd been alive. David picked up the magazine lying between them and cleared his throat. The hard-faced girl used her pinkie to clean lipstick from the corners of her mouth.

"How you want it?" Ming asked Marcy as the girl parted the beads and entered the room, a towel draped over her shoulders, her hair wet and heavy around her face. She held out a magazine picture of a model with gleaming, pin-straight hair. Ming snatched it away and jammed the picture into the side of the mirror. She pumped a bar at the bottom of the chair, raising it a few inches.

First, Ming combed Marcy's hair, yanking her head

backward with each stroke. Then she removed a spiked brush and hair dryer from a hook at the side of the counter and tilted the girl's face upward, scrutinizing her. Sighing, Ming pointed the hair dryer at the picture in the mirror. "No good," she said. "We do my way." Marcy started to protest, then leaned back in the chair.

Scowling, Ming pulled at Marcy's hair. She used some purple goop, then sprayed something from a plastic bottle. Except for an almost imperceptible twitch of the eyelids, Marcy was still. David felt sorry for her. She wanted a different self, but her hairdresser wouldn't allow it.

He watched Ming rotating around the girl. At times Marcy's hair looked awful, stuck with metal pins and plastic clips, but when Ming released a section from its confines, it fluttered down elegantly. Ming worked fast, her mouth set and determined, blonde hair swinging. Her black roots spread from the crown of her head in a star shape.

The sweetness of hairspray made David drowsy. He closed his eyes, daydreaming about the hard-faced girl. He pictured her stepping carefully into her strapless black dress, afraid to muss her hair. Her shoulders were freckled. He saw her sitting stiffly in a chair, looking at a clock.

Marcy was hugging Ming. Her hair was beautiful, still curly, but twisted into long, smooth spirals. She smiled at David.

Bing-Chen

"God Bless America," he said, and whistled.

Ming held up a hand mirror so Marcy could see the back of her hair. The hard-faced girl sat on the couch, legs crossed, licking the tips of her fingers and turning the pages of a magazine. She would be a paradigm First Lady, polished and brisk, MADE IN THE USA labels sewn into her blazers, a compact and travel-size tissues in her purse. When it was her turn to be coiffed, she allowed Ming to swathe her in a plastic apron that snapped shut at the neck like a bib. She looked directly at herself in the mirror, sure of how she would turn out.

David wondered how he appeared to the prom girls. Did they think he was old? Did they know he was Chinese? He had said only three words—for all they knew, he could be fresh off the boat. But no, his shoes and pants were obviously American. And he had no accent. His brown hair graying on the sides; his brown eyes, deep and gathered. Epicanthic folds, his ex-girlfriend, Kerry, a med student, had said.

Sometimes people could not tell he was Chinese; other times it was all they saw. It had always been like that. He suddenly wished he could have the constancy and assurance of Ming and the prom girls. Made of one thing, they knew who they were. So young, and they already knew.

His mother had liked Kerry. They still kept in touch,

sent holiday cards: *Kerry is starting a private practice; she's married; they had a boy.*

When the prom girls left, Ming stood in front of David; "You're uneven on the sides," she tugged on her blonde hair. "I'll fix it. No problem."

Heels tapping forcefully, she led him behind the red beads into a small room. By a filmy window he saw a sink with a scooped neckrest. Shampoos and dyes stacked the shelves above the sink. An olive green hat with a peaked brim hung on the wall. It looked like a Communist cap. To the left of it was a narrow staircase. David saw a pile of folded towels on the bottom step.

When he settled his neck and head in the sink, he was practically lying down. He was surprised when Ming began washing his hair, but he did not ask about her mother.

Vigorously, she scrubbed his head. Her long nails scratched at his scalp, hurting and tickling. David closed his eyes and let her clean him, relaxing as she cradled his head with one hand and rinsed the back of his neck with the other. A breeze from a fan moved the beaded partition. It clicked softly.

He thought of the painting above his mother's bed. As a child, he had liked to look up at it. A snowcapped mountain, deep in wispy clouds. *Shan Shui*, mountain and water landscape—his mother had told him. One day, he realized there was a man in the picture standing with a staff at the base of the mountain. It made him feel strange to think he had looked at the painting for years without ever noticing the tiny figure.

Bing-Chen, Bing-Chen? he could hear his mother calling him. By his name, his Chinese name. She only called him David if she was mad at him—or his father. Sometimes she called him Little Rat. As he had left her apartment earlier in the day she had said, gently: "Things will get better. It's your year, Little Rat."

The smell of peanuts and red-bean paste filled the room. From upstairs, he heard a sizzling, then smelled chicken. Ming was leaving. He should follow her.

She held up her hand, "Stay there. You need more time."

He lay back in the chair, his head resting in the curved sink. The smells here were familiar, homey. His mother cooked chicken with bok choy and straw mushrooms. He looked at the exposed pipes hanging above his head.

Yellow. Laney Carson, his prom date, had worn a yellow dress. He had bought her an orchid.

He remembered the shock on Laney's face when he introduced his mother. "I didn't know you were Japanese," she said. She had blinked.

"Sorry," he answered.

What a stupid thing to say. Sorry. He hadn't even corrected her.

"OK. It's time," Ming said, and led him to the counter. She stepped on a pedal, lowering the chair. This part was always uncomfortable. He didn't know where to look—in the mirror, at the wall? Maybe he should close his eyes.

Ming circled him, tilting his head up and down. She combed his hair forward, then parted it down the middle, drawing her finger up the line of his scalp. Snipping and sighing, muttering and tugging, she moved around him. His hair was black with wetness. She did not seem to be cutting much, just, somehow, shaping.

Switching on the hair dryer, Ming feathered her fingers through David's hair. He closed his eyes and thought of his mother sitting in the same place, the same chair. Her gnarled hands in her lap. Ming was her girl. They probably chatted the entire time, telling stories and jokes.

He didn't want to talk. He wanted to sit there, under the warm stream of air and Ming's light, soft hands.

The hair dryer stopped whirring. David opened his eyes.

His hair was dry, jet black and glossy. Ming had dyed it. It hung around his face in an oval frame.

Bing-Chen

"Looks good," she said and grinned. "Thirty bucks."

Scattered around the chair was a pile of shorn hair, rising slightly in the wind of the oscillating fan. His black, Marcy's brown, the hard-faced girl's red, sprinkles of Ming's blonde. The fluffy heap was like an animal. With a push broom, Ming swept the pile to the side of the room. She straightened the magazines and put the hard-faced girl's check on the counter between a can of Aquanet and a statue of Future Buddha. *Mi-lo Fuo*, who predicted the weather and carried a cloth bag of treats for children.

Yes, he had listened. He remembered some things.

His hair was shiny and even on the sides. He looked younger. Like his mother's first cousin. Ming hadn't asked his permission. But the dye-job did look good.

He would get his mother's newspaper and drop it off on his way home. They would have tea, listen to the radio. She would tell him about the flood near Guilin.

Opening his wallet, David gave Ming forty dollars. "Here," he said. "*Xie-xie*. Thanks."

She lifted a hand in farewell. "*Zai jian.*"

Domestication
of an
Imaginary
Goat

She wanted to sew him a goat, but the idea of it incomplete was unbearable. She would find it, in a drawer, beneath the sweater he had bought for her when she shivered as they walked toward the beach. "Are you cold?" he had asked, and she answered, "I'm all right." He handed her the towels, the umbrella that she could not open by herself if the wind was blowing (that gusty day, years ago, when he had gone to buy lemonades and she opened the umbrella, alone, and it was torn from her hands, had sailed down the beach and landed in the water among the breakers. She dragged it back to their towels; it was sodden, heavy. When he returned, he laughed with his head thrown back, his Adam's apple trotting up and down, the lemonade spilling carelessly over the sides of the paper cups. He opened the umbrella swiftly, with one hand, despite its heaviness, despite the wind, and she drove the cups of lemonade into the sand, liking how the grains stuck to the wet sides in sharp patterns, like *rangoli).* But that was before the sweater. "You look cold," he had said and handed her the goggles, hers with prescription lenses; one could be carefree, careless, when they had never known blindness—she always thought that of him, his unflawed vision and unmarred temperament, and he jogged away. She turned to watch him, his heels kicking up the golden sand, the soles of his feet, white and narrow, jogging to the shops near the parking lot where he bought her a sweater, mauve, a color she did not like, but he had wanted her to be pleased with him, she could see that, she could see what he wanted, and so she smiled and thanked him, and later, when they were home with salty legs and brittle hair, she put the sweater in a drawer, but she never wore it, never; it was mauve, a shade that made her complexion sallow. So she thought, if there was to be an incomplete goat, she would put it under the sweater since she rarely touched it and certainly never looked underneath it. She was not ungrateful; she knew how kind he was, how good. It was simply that she did not like mauve, and he knew that, but he had decided her dislike was unimportant. What was important, he thought, were the simple things: that he noticed she was cold, that he wanted to please her and make her warm. That was all true — she agreed. But she did not like that he had decided. She would not change her mind. She did not like mauve, and that mattered.

But perhaps beneath the sweater was too obvious a place for an incomplete goat. Perhaps she should put the goat somewhere darker, a space that was less likely to be often encountered, like the closet full of spare soaps, saline solutions, hotel shampoos, boxes of tissues, and detergent. A bottle of detergent could last six months, and there were already two in that closet (not to mention the full bottle on top of the dryer) which, all told, would account for a year and a half. If the incomplete goat were shoved behind the bottle of detergent, it could be forgotten for at least a year and a half. And maybe, after she used the bottle on top of the dryer and the first bottle from the closet, she would feel compelled to buy more detergent, for she liked to have two of everything. She despised needing something and not having it, not preparing for the eventuality of necessity or fancy, especially because *he* never prepared for anything, not for loss or expenditure or the depletion of household resources. (That would make him laugh, her saying, "the depletion of household resources.") She had a list, of course, every organized person has more than a few, but when she sent him shopping he would forget the list and buy what he thought would please her. It was not hard to figure out what pleased her. He only had to pay attention. If he paid attention, he would know what she liked, and more importantly, what she did not like, but he was drifting, dreaming (and that was why she would make him a goat. One night, a few weeks ago, they had seen an orange, spreading light in the sky, toward New Jersey; she knew it was man-made, a satellite, a test explosion near the air force base, but he thought it was something magnificent, never seen before, like God or aliens, so convinced he was, so excited, as if this was the moment he had been waiting for, the moment when something extraordinary happened, when he was selected for greatness, and then she had mocked him and called him a Space Goat—the name had just burst from her and they had known what it meant, known it was appropriate, for he was always drifting, dreaming, out of this world) and so at the store, he bought what he thought would please her and was hurt when she grimaced. And then she would feel sorry and force a smile, and say "Thank you," but with her eyes averted, and she would hate the clutter the things he thought would please her created in the closets and drawers.

But how sweet of him to try. He couldn't help his drifting any more than she could help her organization. How good of him to want to please her, to ask for her approval. How good of him to love her. And so she would not begin the goat, for fear that she would not finish it, fearing the reason (the only one—once she began something, she always finished it; it was part of her organization), the only reason that would cause her not to finish the goat: that he would be gone. That there would be no one to give the goat to. That there would be no one who liked to please her, to make her warm, for she had driven him away, had asked a dreamer with a cheerful temperament to be organized. Demanded it. When what she liked best about him was his drifting, his imagination, his attraction to clutter and the spur of the moment. How easily he laughed and dragged her out of her tidiness, her adherence to duty. If he was gone, there would be no reason to finish the goat, and it would be shoved, incomplete, under the mauve sweater or behind the third bottle of detergent, to be discovered in a year and a half, maybe two.

The thought of the unfinished goat was impossible. One day she would find it. That was what she could not bear. What combinations of incompleteness would the goat suffer from? A head, and no body? Three lanky legs and two gangly horns, unpointed and limp because she had run out of stuffing? Stuffing for a cloth goat was not something she knew how to prepare for. Perhaps it would have only one eye? No mouth? A creature with no mouth is a terrible thing. Worse than one without eyes. Why was that, she wondered? What is it about a mouth? She had seen a painting, once, of a woman without a mouth. The woman had small eyes, with long lashes, black hair, ears shaped like shells, the suggestion of breasts, large ones, beneath a blue blouse, fingernails even, and a wedding ring. But there was no mouth. The painting was terrifying. The woman had no mouth. Where it should have been was a smooth, flesh-colored space, as if skin had grown over the mouth, as if the woman had been born without one. It would have been better to see lips sewn shut, or stapled. The benign absence of the mouth was horrible.

She stood looking at the painting until a man and his girlfriend (girlfriend, because she, too, had no ring on her finger) stood next to her, and the girlfriend said to the man, "She has no mouth," and the man responded, "I'd like to paint yours out sometimes," and he had meant it, he had really meant it, and the girlfriend had been ashamed. Not that he had said it, but because a stranger, a woman, had overheard him.

She had moved away from the painting then. A creature without a mouth—a goat, a woman—is ashamed, mutilated. But the words that sometimes come from the mouth. From her own mouth. Those could be horrible, too.

Domestication of an Imaginary Goat

She did not want to buy him a present; she wanted to make him one. It had not been difficult in the past: she made roses out of metal funnels and pipe cleaners and green sandpaper cut into leaves. She had made a hedgehog once (before he was a Space Goat he had been a Sleepy Hedgehog) out of a sea sponge and nails and drill bits and mini-wrenches that she had taken from the emergency toolbox in the trunk of her car (because if there ever was an emergency, she would not know how to use the wrenches, she would stand there with them in her hands, her face lit by the emergency flares he insisted she stow under the passenger seat, but even with the flares, the wrenches, she would not know how to solve the problem). Now she wanted to make a goat. To sew it. But then there was the idea of it unfinished.

What if she vowed (to herself—those are the only vows that matter) that if the goat had to be discarded before it was complete, she would push the needle she had used to sew it, and the green thread (for the thread would be dark green, she had already picked it out, already purchased it—she hated the thought of a white goat, she wouldn't make it white just because it was supposed to be white), she would push the needle—the dark green thread looped through it and umbilically attached to the incomplete goat—into the fabric (sea green with small red and yellow

171

flowers: a green goat with budding skin), poke it into the fabric so the bright, shiny steel of the needle laced through the cloth, and then, yes, she would promise herself to throw out the goat, the needle, the thread, the spare scraps of fabric, the black-button eyes, the beanbag stuffing, the plastic orb (she had bought a tin ring from a machine outside of the grocery store. The ring came in a plastic orb that she knew would fit around the head of the goat, an astronaut's helmet so that the goat could be transformed into a Space Goat—he would appreciate that sort of detail, that type of whimsy. She knew what he liked. She knew how to please him). She would throw it all out in a garbage can, far from the apartment, so there would be no chance for nostalgia, no doubling back, no rummaging frantically through the can as if her life depended on recovering the goat, for if she threw it all out in a garbage can, far away, she would never find the incomplete goat, and upon finding it, remember how she had sewn it—for him—how she had hoped. And it was this idea of a goat, forgotten, symbolic, that prevented her from ever beginning, and so the dark green thread, the fabric, the button eyes, the stuffing remained inside a paper bag deep under the bed so he would not find them if he happened to lift the dust ruffle, which he rarely did, unless he lost a shoe or a sock.

• • •

Domestication of an Imaginary Goat

The idea of the goat frightened him. Mostly, it was her face (how open it could be, how unprotected) when she talked of the goat. She asked him if he liked the name, Yama (she laughed, and shouted, Yama, Goat of Death, her thin fingers spread wide), and when she shouted, he was reminded of first meeting her, years ago; she approached him, a stranger then, standing outside of the Chelsea post office, and asked which idea he liked better: museums filled with beds, you could pick what kind of sheets you wanted, flannel, silk, cotton, stretched taut over a single, double, queen- or king-size bed (it would be all about choices, the museum, choices and comfort) and the art would hang from the ceiling; or, an adult playground with slides and swings and seesaws, where grown-ups could wail, stand in sprinklers, and throw tantrums for no reason (it would be all about release and joy). He liked that she shouted, but sometimes he wished she wouldn't, for what did people think when they saw a thirty-five-year-old woman shouting about a goat. (He had preferred the playground; the idea of her growling and pushing him down a slide made him laugh.) It was what he liked about her. Her ideas. Her childishness. But how easily she was hurt. It always surprised him.

Sometimes he wondered if it was time and work that held two people together. He had tried to say the words the way she wanted him to: *garro*, Hyderabad, *sai bhaji*, *Guea me sura.* If he said them incorrectly, she called him a *ghati*, and laughed uproariously, savoring the full meaning of a word he had never heard before. The places she talked about, far away, not even part of his imagination. And then she had told him about her grandmother, about her grandmother's wealth, her short, modern hair (Sindhis do as they please, she said; we're a wild bunch), and how the old woman, honored for her age and ability to tell the story of everyone's birth and death, save her own, would milk thirty *bakri*, thirty goats, every day before dawn (in her white sari, *manik* necklace, and a man's brown derby). He had learned to make *loli* the way her grandmother did, had learned to say "Partition" with bite, with loss in the voice. But then she had started with the goat. And he hadn't been ready.

What do you think of goats? she had asked. They're great, he said. Yes, they are, she agreed, and went on to describe a house they would have (one day), and land (always, she talked about land) with a small, fierce stream running through it, and she would beat his shirts on the rocks even though she hadn't done that in India (there were dhobis for that). Can't you just see it! she said, and we will have a goat, she said, and he will drink from the stream and crop the grass with his rectangle teeth and you will never have to mow the lawn, but you must fence off my herb garden and protect it from the goat; I will grow tulsi,

Domestication of an Imaginary Goat

for Girdhir, Lifter of the Mountain, and Guru Nanak. He
had not wanted to think of a house they would one day live
in, and she saw that, and it made her more persistent and
she said All right, then we won't speak of the land or the
house, but at least tell me what you would want to name
the goat (I will make cheese! she shouted, forgetting that
she had called the goat "he"), and she was persisting,
pressing, and he felt himself pursued by horns, by cleft
hooves and swinging udders, and she grew desperate and
hurt (he could always see it in the skin around her nose—
it shrunk, and he knew then, she was hurt. She said her
nose was Sindhi, with pride and sadness, but hers was the
only Sindhi nose he knew, and he could not share in her
pride or sadness, although he did like her nose). Just tell
me what you would name the goat, she said, or tell me if
you would want a white goat, brown or black or speckled.
Just imagine the goat, it's not real, just imagine it, and he
knew he could reverse her hurt if he would just agree to
imagine the goat, it was not so much for her to ask, really,
he knew that, but she was pushing, he could see the
forelock of the goat, could smell its hot, grassy breath,
could feel it nipping, unraveling the hem in his trousers,
and there she was now conjuring a hammock, now a
screened-in porch, now making him tea the way she did
with cloves and milk and bringing it to him as he sat

outside with the goat, and then suddenly there was a child and she named it herself, did not even ask him, gave it a name, Usha, and a sex, girl, and sat it on his knee while he taught her to fix carburetors (she wanted a girl who could fix carburetors and play the tabla, or a boy who danced ballet and Kuchipudi), and all the while the goat looked on, cropping the grass so that he did not have to mow, but he had always liked mowing, why couldn't he mow if he wanted to? And he began to resent the goat for doing what he wanted to do, began to resent that goat for existing in his imagination, and now she was naming it, calling it Yama, Goat of Death, with her long, pretty fingers spread wide. (How the tendons showed, how narrow her nailbeds, how fast she rolled-out dough and sprinkled *rangoli* when she was especially land-sick, as she called it. Sindhis must make their home where they are, she said, we are not homeless, only landless, like so many others.) He did learn his lessons well, after all; he loved that she let him shuffle through the *rangoli*, destroy it, for that was the point, that destruction is part of life, eventually it comes to all, even goats, even children named Usha, nations and borders, the Amil neighborhood in Hyderabad, Sindh, before Partition—said with bite and loss—even houses and fierce streams and rocks. He did think Yama a good name for a goat, especially a goat that butted into his business, but he would not say so, for to say so would be to play along with the game, her game, to admit that he too could imagine the goat, and if he could imagine the goat, then of course she would go on to the next thing, she would not let it go at the goat, she would demand that he imagine the land, the house, the child named Usha (Dawn, she explained, it means dawn, with that look that excluded him, that meant she was remembering something outside of him. He had read somewhere that "exclusion" was the dirtiest word in the English language). She would know that he could envision the hammock and porch swing (*Arrey, jhoola*, she said, *tweek-a-tweek*), the tea, sweet and hot in his mouth, and so he shouted at her, saw the skin near her Sindhi nose that made her so proud and sad, shrink. He shouted: "I don't want the damn goat! Get rid of it!" And then he started to laugh, he threw his head back and laughed, and he was glad when she began to laugh too, because sometimes he would laugh and she would rage or weep, but this time they laughed together for fighting over a goat that did not exist.

The
Rigors of
Dance Lessons

I see my wife squatting on the ground, looking for something.

"What is it?" I call to her, and she answers me simply: "I have lost you."

In body, she is not herself but an old man wearing the collar of a priest and a fishing hat. The hat is stuck with metal lures that glint and tinkle. Over the ground, her hands skim quickly. She will not look up at me.

"Well," I say, "don't worry, I'll help," and drop down beside her. "Where did you last see me?"

She points to a building I had not noticed. I look away from the spiny white whiskers pushing through her chin.

"Why don't we look in there?"

"There's more light out here," she says. I am chastened.

She turns and grabs me by the earlobes, shouting, "Dance lessons! Dance lessons! That's what we need!" Shaking my finger at her, I say, "You took too long. We'll miss the lesson."

"No. *You* won't," she says, and smiles.

We sit against a mirrored wall in a room with wood floors. In a corner I see the flip-flops I bought her ten years ago. In another corner, stacked on a white plate, are the cupcakes she baked for me last week. The room is filled with little girls in patent-leather tap shoes. There is one boy. Dressed in a tuxedo, he sits next to me. "They're sisters," he says, pointing at two women, one dark-skinned, one light, looking out a window.

"Are you here for the lesson?" I ask.

"No," he says. His ruffled shirt is yellowed; his pant legs end just above his ankles. A red bow tie wilts from his thin neck. He resembles the older and darker of the sisters. They share a tautness around the nostrils and upper lip. Both are dark-skinned with crisp, black eyes. The boy's hair needs to be cut, and the woman's is wound into a tight bun held in place by two enormous gold sticks stuck in the shape of a cross. A man and guitar wail from a tape player balanced on the windowsill.

"Gypsies," my wife whispers to me. The metal lures shake from her hat. While I looked at the boy, she aged. Her hair has changed from grey to white, and the whiskers on her chin have grown into a cropped beard. She says, "When I was a boy in Cairo, one stole a fig right out of my mouth."

"I remember that," answers the boy in the tuxedo. He leans over me to shake my wife's hand. "Do you think he'll like flamenco?" He sounds concerned.

"I hope so," she says.

The light-skinned sister begins clapping. She wears her blonde hair loose. Beneath her purple dress, ruffled in layers like birthday cake, her body is young, full. Her sister sits behind her in a wooden chair, clapping at the same beat. "Come on, children; join us," she calls, and we do. Suddenly, the two sisters stamp between their claps, the dark one so quickly, she has stamped three times before her sister's hands come together once. Eyes closed, the dark woman sways in the chair, a soft "*Olé*" slipping from her dry lips. The little girls clap earnestly and tap their patent-leather feet.

"Watch," the boy says to me and stamp-shuffles into the center of the room, clapping with his hands held next to his head and his body twisted to the left. He wears high-heeled shoes, and a tasseled sash around his waist. His two front teeth protrude. The two sisters clap faster, prompting him with *olé*'s and hearty stomps. I laugh as the boy makes some tentative movements with his hips and a few striking stamps, as if killing spiders. After each strike with his high-heeled shoes, the boy tilts his head and considers, nodding slowly to himself. As he pounds out a rapid staccato and whirls around the light sister, his exposed ankles flash.

The light sister moves to one side of the room, and the boy's mouth becomes cocky and boastful. I laugh again and clap louder. "That's right," the light sister shouts to me, "You've got it!" With each stamp, humor slams down the boy's legs. I notice he keeps his toes on the floor to make the stamps louder. I slam my heels against the floor. "More passion," the dark sister shouts to me, "Keep your hips under your shoulders." I am still sitting down; I am sweating. The boy shuffles comically off to the side. He is replaced in the center of the room by the dark sister in a yellow dress.

"You idiot," she says to the boy. "He hasn't learned anything." A cleavage of bones shows in her scooped bodice. When she dances, I cry. The woman stomps with machismo, her chest puffed out, her legs held wide. She seems to oppose the air around her and scowls at herself in the mirrored wall. She moves faster, provoking and challenging with each heave of her arms, shock of her feet whipping against the polished wood floors. I know she is trying to show us, the children—but no, I am not a child—how to dance, but I am afraid of her anger, her certainty. "Do I keep my toes in or out?" I whisper. The dark woman ignores me. Her legs flurry up and down like pistons, and the cross at the back of her bun wiggles as she snaps her head high in a final flourish. I weep and sniffle a little. My wife shoves me and laughs. "That one was not for you," she says.

And now the macho sister joins the humorous boy and together they lean against a wall. The light woman hesitates in the center of the room, waiting till they work themselves into a clapping, stamping empathy, and then she dances, dances with a light exuberance, her strikes against the floor more like playful taps than the hammering of the other two. Her pleasure in her own legs and arms delights me. "Is this for me?" I whisper to my wife. The boy shouts at me, "You never listen! She wants you to turn your feet out! Not in, never in!"

The light sister keeps her torso still, forcing all the movement and expression into her hips and knees, elbows and wrists. She is content with me, with herself, with this room. She seems to be saying how uncomplicated this dream could be, with the right attitude and a good pair of legs. Her hair flings around her like a cape. When a question creases her forehead, I understand—a concern that she will not always be so free. "Is it my fault?" I wonder out loud. Her joy returns and she rattles her legs, smoothing the worry away. She stops in the center of the room, poised like a ceramic pitcher, one hand on her hip, one arm curved above her head. The boy switches off the tape.

"Your turn," my wife says. I am nervous. The little girls snicker behind their hands. Standing, I try to dance like the boy, like the macho and light sister. "No," the boy reprimands, "be like us one at a time." I can feel my wife watching me. I want to wear her hat; I want to shred her collar into little pieces. I sit down, tired from so much dancing. My wife will not look at me. Leaning over, I bite her cheek. Her head has turned to chocolate. Horrified, I scream. I am not afraid of her chocolate cheek. She is hollow and hollowness scares me. No caramel, no cream, just air.

"What have you done?" I ask her.

"Made room for you," she says.

"Do you have enough room for yourself?"

"Yes. I think so."

"I get tired keeping my hips beneath my shoulders." I say it softly. I do not want to hurt her.

"I get tired watching for your feet." When my wife says this, she is the boy in the tuxedo.

The Rigors of Dance Lessons

I am ashamed that I wanted her hat.
"Don't worry," she says, and offers me a cupcake.
We are fine; she has had this dream before, too.

Bolero

War: Euskal Herria

His mother opens the curtain (as a girl she embroidered green blades of grass along the bottom seam) and says to Felix: I was happy here.

The boy sits up in bed and sees that she has powdered her eyelids, steel. The color reaches to the black line of her brows and two circles of rouge target her cheeks. He knows she is leaving.

Felix, honey, she says and tousles his hair, Don't be a goosey. Your grandfather will teach you about music and sheep.

Against his scalp, her fingers are cold and the underside of her wrist smells of lilac.

Where the Long Grass Bends

Good-bye, he says.

In a while, Crocodile, she singsongs, Honest Injun.

In the beginning, refugees straggle up the road to France. They travel by night, shedding property: a weighty urn, a pair of shoes, a dogeared *Cántico* by Jorge Guilen that Felix brings home in the waist of his pants.

The boy learns to play the piano, flute, and *alboka*, two animal horns joined by a mouthpiece. But the violin is still his favored instrument. He cradles it, trailing the sheep over scanty paths, and drapes himself across the back of an old ewe to practice scales. His grandfather shows him how to jig his fingers, to bump and drag the bow. Tempo, Aitor tells the boy, is a heartbeat. Music, too, needs to live.

They clean sheep manure from the heels of their boots. The front door flings open; church bells clang from the north. A woman wearing a black shawl steps into the house. *Aviones! Aviones!* she shouts and leaves.

Aitor throws water on the fire, leans out the door, and whistles. Glancing at the sky, he sees a squadron of planes flying south toward the village. When the dog pushes past his legs, he shuts the door. Felix turns down the gas lamps, pulls the shutters closed. And as he, Aitor, and the dog huddle under the stout dinner table, the first wave of planes sweep the house. The roof shudders. In the cabinets, the plates and glasses quake.

The initial bombing is fast. Through the patter of spraying dirt, Felix hears the rooster crow from the henhouse. (I forgot to latch the screen, he says.) Aitor grips the legs of the table and watches the clock. They hear planes dropping close again and the drumming of heavy bombs. The wood floor buckles beneath them, the shutters flap and groan. Aitor rasps a thumb over his chin (my heart, Felix thinks, will pump from my chest), and then they hear the planes turning, coming back. There is a shriek, spanning three octaves. A rumble. The house tilts, the cabinet doors burst open, and plates shatter on the floor. Be calm, be calm, Felix tells the dog.

On his hands and knees, Aitor crawls from under the table and grabs Felix's violin. He orders the boy to stand (Up, Up) and drags him to the piano. At first Felix struggles (Let me go; the dog is frightened), then he takes the violin from his grandfather and holds it to his chest. Aitor pulls out the piano bench. They hear the fence splinter and the sheep snorting in panic.

Play! Aitor commands, and lays his fingers on the piano keys, sounding the introductory phrase of *Violinsonaten in C minor*, Beethoven. Uneasy, Felix and his violin join in late, an untuned semiquaver, a sixteenth note accompaniment.

Where the Long Grass Bends

There is a battering at the front door, and it falls inward with a bang. The dog barks steadily. A few sheep skitter into the house, and Felix notices a buzz on his D string.

The piano part veers away from the violin; the violin pursues, struts, and for a few bars they twine together. From Aitor's left hand, a torrent of chords; the violin flits away. Felix leans into his chin rest. Under the table, the dog cowers as bricks course down the chimney. The lamps sputter and smoke. Down, down the keyboard, Aitor's right hand chases his left, and finally the confrontation of the first movement, the butting of heads, like two warring sheep.

When they begin the second movement, *adagio*, the roof is shaking (it will fly off, twirl away, Felix thinks) and sheep are streaming through the front door. They defecate on the floor, bleating and knocking over chairs. The wind, bilious, thick, follows the sheep inside, and the dog splits the flock, herding half upstairs and bunching the other half in a corner, behind the padded chairs. Felix and Aitor play on, fingers running, arms pumping. The piano unfurls a *cadenza*; the violin answers with fitful chops. The clock topples and splits open, scattering silver gears.

Allegretto, they launch into the third movement, the music kicking up its heels, a few sheep lying down. Night comes on and the darkness inside purples. Machine guns strafe the windows, cracking the glass in jigsaw shapes. The dog nips at the sheep, bundling them closer together. The lamps throw shadows onto the wall behind the piano, and Felix sees a horse with a spike for a tongue. In miniature, nervous darts, Aitor's fingers strike the keys and then, together, piano and violin play through the finale.

The boy lays down his instrument and wipes his palms. At the base of the stairs, he sees an unfamiliar grey cat. Do you know what that was? Aitor says hoarsely, wading through a haze of ash and plaster. He pushes Felix back under the table. They sit on the dust of obliterated bricks, and Aitor says, That was defiance. Felix begins to cry, Where is the dog, he sobs, I left the latch up, and his grandfather soothes: It's all right, everything's fine.

Through the gaping front door they see an old sheep, its fleece on fire. As it clatters up the front steps, it is gunned down. A duck wanders inside and dies near the stairs. The hills are black and trees flare like candles. The sky flashes with pale yellow lights. Music fills Felix's head, the beat of planes, the reedy spill of bombs. The grey cat, bleeding from its ears, shakes the duck twice, then drops it.

Evolution

When he finds the pregnant ewe, Felix swings the lantern, calling, Here, Here. Her throat is ripped open, and blood covers the ground in frozen rills. With a knife, Aitor slices at her belly and drags the lamb out. Slick from his mother's death and his own new life, the lamb freezes to the ground. It will die, Aitor says, but we'll do our best.

To cut a circle in the ice, they use an axe. The sound of the hacking is high, metallic. The lamb opens his gummy mouth, wheezes; his visible eye flickers. The skin on Felix's fingers shreds as he helps his grandfather pry the slab from the ground. They lift the thick circle of ice, the lamb adhered to it, and see a wolf standing under a pear tree.

Let him finish, Aitor says, This winter has been hard for all of us.

A new clock, a wooden birdhouse, hangs above the stove. On the hour, the roof pops up and a cardinal with green glass eyes and a leather tongue sings "Claire de Lune." Felix whistles along with the bird. His grandfather's omelets taste the same as his mother's: buttery, browned, and sprinkled with grated cheese.

She was right to name you for Mendelssohn, his grandfather says.

The sheep mill around Felix, their ropy shag tangled with twigs. It is part of the boy's duties to groom the wool, to keep it clean and loose, but on this day he feels idle. He lies on his back, watching the wind shove clouds across the sky, the violin rising and falling on his stomach.

In the next pasture, over a low stone wall, a brown pony bucks. The smell of manure is sweet, and lying there, Felix isolates sounds: the thudding of the pony's hooves, her gait on grass (spongy) and on packed dirt (grumose), the clacking jaws of the sheep, the mushy wallop of wind in his ears.

Standing, he tucks the violin under his chin and holds the bow in place above the strings. He dribbles his fingers up the fingerboard, splays his feet. A pear falls from a tree. Felix plays. The violin ululates. He holds the bow low in his palm, freeing his fingers to *pizzicato*. The pony streaks around the field, her blonde tail and mane flying, and Felix matches his bowing to her pace. Faster and faster, he plays a cycle of notes, the music shaped like a ball, like the path of the pony, and then Felix lifts the bow up, away from the strings.

He points the bow at a sheep. It bleats. The bow sweeps toward the sky, and the wind huffs. To the trees the bow arches and a bird twits. Felix knows he is not causing the sounds; he is anticipating them. Warm and solid, the sheep press against him, nosing at his back. He looks at the brown pony, her ribbony mane and tail: the hair of his bow is alive and streams out from his hand, galloping.

Finding a stick with a bulbous end, Felix picks it up.

He holds the small knob, lightly, between his right thumb and forefinger, and uses the stick as a baton to keep the meter of the dropping pears, the wind, the pony, brisk and buoyant. And later, as the sun sets in an orange sky and the sheep, growing restless, rub their black faces against his legs, he drops the stick and uses only his hands to conduct.

Time Passes

Felix buries his grandfather in a pine box under the pear trees (he finds the coffin, filled with spare shears and a broken flute, in the attic). He dons Aitor's beret, takes the bus into Gernika and sends his mother a telegram: *Atr dead. Pls Come. Yrs Flx.*

When she comes, she sells the herd, the house, the piano, the orchard. A mink snuggles against her neck. They drive to Barcelona. She takes Felix to Parc Guell where they walk a passage cut into a hillside. The ceiling of the promenade leans fiendishly, reminding Felix of ribs. Pillars plummet from the ceiling, like tree trunks, growing down. Hearing the cooing of doves, the boy feels the gash of his grief sealing over. The place is like Stravinsky, turned to stone. Absently, his mother strokes the flattened ears of her mink.

She says: You're going to the new Julliard School of

Bolero

Music, it's what your grandfather said you wanted, he made me promise to sell the land and the house to fund your education. He said you were a great musician who happened to love sheep. And I am sorry about the flock, I know you are sad, and I know that you blame me for leaving. Her voice echoes through the hall. Felix counts the repetitions.

His mother walks ahead of him to the car. In the trunk are his violin and a suitcase full of clothes. Felix takes his grandfather's beret from his head and wears it on his knee. They drive by Sagrada Familia, the unfinished spires, riddled with holes.

Years later, when Felix is a guest conductor for the Baltimore Symphony Orchestra, a Spanish cellist tells him what she saw in Pablo Picasso's living room—a huge panettone, chewed to ruin by mice. What is it? she asked Picasso, and spitefully, with relish, he answered: Gaudi's Model.

The first time Felix jumped a horse (the same brown pony with blonde mane and tail) it refused a two-foot wall. His grandfather told him, You must put the horse in the correct frame of mind. Then it will carry you over.

What is an orchestra, if not a huge animal, or pack of animals that must be put in the correct frame of mind?

Where the Long Grass Bends

When conducting, Felix has his strings practice unified bowing. Think like a mob, he tells them, Be like a crowd with one idea. Woodwinds and brass practice breath control to sustain long passages: Sounds mealy, he admonishes. Militaristic, that's the key. Without precision, emotion is drippy. His rehearsals are laborious: Bow sparingly on the G, For bar 223, stay in the middle, Play the next passage stately, *legato*, Sing, sing like a bicycle racing uphill, For God's Sake, Do NOT drop the C# *appoggiatura* or we will start again, The beat is wrong, go Ba-DUM-DUM-DUM-da-da, not BA-dum-DUM-dum-da-DA.

Jean-Baptiste Lully, the *Maître de musique* at the court of Louis XIV, used a staff as tall as himself and topped by a jeweled crown to keep time. A human metronome, he pounded his stick against the floor so his beats would be heard by the orchestra. While directing a Te Deum to celebrate His Majesty's recovery from an illness, Lully, in a powdered wig, high-heeled buckled shoes, and frilly ruff, was overcome. Rapping forcefully upon the stage with his staff, he accidentally stabbed himself in the foot. The wound he suffered proved to be gangrenous. On his deathbed, he composed a hymn, "Sinner, Thou Must Die," and sang it for friends.

Bolero

. . .

After the Communist Revolution, Russian conductors directed without a baton, and in 1922, Moscow's preeminent orchestra eliminated the role of conductor. This communal, socialist symphony came to be known as *Persimfans*. Musicians were expected to conduct themselves. *Persimfans* perished in a few short weeks.

Felix loves these two stories.

Again, My Heart

When Felix sees Ilona vaulting over the backs of velvet seats in Carnegie Hall, a sheaf of music clamped between her teeth, he feels no paternity, no lust, nothing but recognition. At the time, she is thirty-seven and Felix, sixty-five. Raising both of his hands, he calls out, Again, my brave strings, from the beginning! and waits for Ilona, his mezzo-soprano, to arrive.

As she hauls herself ungracefully on stage, he clucks at her feet in flat sandals. A grey dress, strapless and cotton, wraps around her like a towel. In the future, you'll be punctual, he says, and purses his lips at the timpanist for missing a cue.

Ilona is short, built like a gourd with a shaved head and

a face full of angles. At the tip, her hooked nose shines. In the plain dress, she reminds Felix of a monk with a violent face, formed cataclysmically, like mountains.

Why are you late? he asks. The orchestra entrance was locked; I had to come through the auditorium. She gestures behind her at the velvet seats but looks directly at him. He feels the same sweep of recognition. Nodding, he raises his hands: Again, my brave strings, from the beginning! In a grieved voice he adds, Viola, viola, I heard no viola.

Ilona stands on stage, beside the timpani, and rubs the back of her head. To warm up, I'll sing Malcom, from *La donna del lago*, aria *Mura felici*, she says. Just so you know, I'm not actually a mezzo-soprano, but a contralto. You have a range of more than three octaves? Felix asks. Yes, high notes like a soprano, low notes like an alto, and the technique to sing coloratura. I sing with three voices. A Trinity, says Felix, Malcom, it is then, the lovestruck man.

Ilona clenches her fists, opens her mouth and works it into a line, a circle, a hexagon. With her fists, she raps lightly on her stomach and looks at Felix, who stares at the strings. Seven measures before the solo, *Atto Primo*, he says, lifting an eyebrow.

There is a rustle of scores, the scrape of music stands and chairs. The strings introduce Ilona. She waits for Felix

Bolero

to glance at her and jab with his left hand, and then, she closes her eyes and sings.

Her voice punches from her mouth, sliding between a baritonelike treble and a piercing soprano. She keeps her fists clenched at her sides and her eyes closed, but responds to all of Felix's directives as if she can see him. Her lips are tan and malleable, and Felix is aware of the fixed instrument mouths that surround her: the trumpet spout, grimacing bass, round flute.

At the close of the aria Felix asks her: Have you ever sung Rosina? Yes, she answers, drawing back her lips to reveal a set of skewed teeth, She's a tricky little strumpet, isn't she? The orchestra laughs along with Felix, and the timpanist gives Ilona a drumroll. They begin rehearsing the performance piece, *Un Ballo in Maschera*, Ilona singing the part of Ulrica, a witch. The character and tempo of Verdi suit her, and she, in gratitude, with joy, directs her voice at the ceiling.

After the first act, Felix lifts his hands toward Ilona and calls out, Again, my heart, from the beginning! Throwing back her head, she closes her eyes, her sharp chin pointing to Felix. She sings, hunched like a gerbil, the tip of her nose shining, the threat of her brawny shoulders rising with her breaths. She reacts to the whisper of bows on wire, currents of air between Felix's conducting hands. It is as if he pulls the sound, the tones from her body. Both of their mouths form the same words as he whispers along with her.

Translations

Naked, Ilona is a violin. Her knobbish ears, shoulders at right angles to neck, her dipped waist, and shining, brown flesh. You are made of eighty pieces, Felix says, bumping a finger down the center of her back. Frets, like a Renaissance fiddle. He rubs her shaved head; it feels like a handful of beach.

Did you know that Alexander Scriabin painted his piano, each key corresponding to a color: C red, G orange, D yellow, and so on?

Yes, Felix answers, I'd heard that. Georgia O'Keeffe also patterned sound. Me, I hear animals. The ratio of mulish oboes to ursa tubas must be balanced, for mules and bears do not thrive in the same environment, and a group of bears will devour a pack of mules. The tuba has more tooth and claw and pound. Although it will never be as spry or dependable as the oboe. The bassoon is my sole mythic. In it, I hear a centaur, not as instructive or owllike as the French horn, more prophetic.

I see, I see.

About ten years ago, I heard Bernstein give a lecture

where he claimed a movement is the equivalent of a sentence. He gave an equation for the translation of music to language: note = phoneme; motive = morpheme; phrase = word; section = clause; movement = sentence; piece = piece.

Do you agree?

No, but he said one thing that I cannot forget.

Tell me.

He said when a phrase is heard more than once, repetition becomes expected, and when that expectation is violated, you have variation. The violation is the variation.

Makes sense.

Yes; I listened to Beethoven's *Pastorale* and this is what I heard: The lark sings yellow tunes, the book is open in the grass, the lark sings yellow tunes, ants cross page eighty-four, the book, the grass, the ant, the frosty trees are green in summer.

Hm.

I am afraid of the dark, Ilona, so you must leave the light on.

You're joking.

No, I fear the dark; I am too easily engulfed.

For one so old, you are young.

For one so young, you are old.

Your heart is beating quickly.

Is it?

My mother, also named Ilona, was Kutchi, a gypsy. She left me pebbles in the soil, black ribbons strung from trees, and I was to recognize her in them, to translate, follow for miles and miles, and find her. The gypsies, she always said, are lost sheep, wandering in search of a flock.

I was once a shepherd, and I have found you.

Your face, when you said that.

An orchestra tuning up is a herd of sheep, reluctant to move, frightened.

We, Ilona and Ilona, came to New York when I was ten. My father was Turkish. He died in Topkapi Palace. We walked from Rajasthan to see the clocks. It was too much for him. Where did you get this scar?

My village, twenty kilometers from Gernika, was bombed.

You were alive then?

Go jump in a lake.

When you are with me, Ilona, how do you feel?

Like I'm listening to Liszt. And your feeling for me?

Korsakov.

In many ways we are the same.

We are not the same. You don't fear the dark, Ilona; you can walk inside it without being lost.

Then everything has been said, everything of

importance, all of this will tug forever between us, an undertow, repeated perhaps in different cities, with different words, but the same, nonetheless. We have spoken.

Scheherazade, Op. 35, *Rimsky-Korsakov*

It begins with the voice of Shahryar. Eleven plodding strokes from the bass, descending in a warning, snakish rattle: this is how to identify him. Now, a pause, a silence. And the scale of change, the ascension of flutes. They ring twice, preparing Shahryar for the entrance of his latest wife.

Here is Scheherezade, not as she sounds when she haggles for the ripest melons, nor as she sounds when she calls to her father, the Grand Vizier, to join her while she feeds the ducks, for she has not seen him all day and cherishes his company. This is the girl's voice, *altissimo*, pulsing with the desire to live—a violin fueled by a loose wrist, clean draws, and perpendicular arm. But do not be fooled, for she is not without guile. It is easy to hear: a strumming harp, disarming against her violin voice. And so Scheherezade is made entirely of strings, and no hand but her own plays them.

Mostly, she sings alone, but sometimes with other bodies of wood and steel. Scheherezade did not learn all of her stories from books, although she is always reading. She collects the tales (strums them) from people. Some she has gathered from the woman who plaits her hair, some from the sweeper's niece who defeathers the chickens, a few from the old gardener who was once a sailor and before that a soldier, and who has circled the globe thrice. Like every storyteller, she is a scavenger: her eyelashes, commas; her lips, parenthetical. It is said she will deliver the daughters of the kingdom, Insh'Allah.

Night after night, her stories continue, Scheherezade falling silent at the approach of dawn and the most beguiling point in her tale. She narrates (the King buries his nose in her hair at the height of coitus) until she has told all she knows.

She says to the King: My mind is empty. He smiles and envisions a green bowl.

Hear the strings plucked as one, a flock of hummingbirds.

September 11, 2001

Ilona cries like a trombone. Felix hears the static and ring of tinnitus. She makes *kadu*. Still, we must eat, she says, but he hears only the ringing and ringing. The stench blows in through the windows. She eats to live. He hears the ringing and pushes the rice around his plate.

Bolero

Felix on the Subway Platform: Halloween

A child in a Superman cape asks his mother: "What does invincible mean?"

"That you can't be hurt." The mother tips the child's face, so he looks up at her.

"Why—do you think you're invincible?"

He ponders. Fingers his cape, picks at his blue tights: "No."

A woman dressed as Nancy Reagan says to her friend, Elvira. "It was an inhuman act."

Ah, but it *was* human. Human made, human caused, human inflicted and suffered.

I cannot listen to music, cannot bear the sound. Ilona hides inside a Mets cap and removes her gypsy bangles. She can read nothing but poetry.

Ilona at the Met

In the crowd at Topkapi Palace
my father said: "I feel Turkish."
I remember the room of clocks,
ticking in tune,
Swiss, German, and French.

Where the Long Grass Bends

Here, in New York,
I stand in front of a small statue,
a man in a nightgown
of handblown glass.
The man has one blue, glass arm
(Jai Shyam)
and one brown.
I am kin to both,
mismatched
and free
of 18th-century portraits,
a population with white,
small hands.

The man in the nightgown
has no lid to his porcelain skull.
He is brainless, indecent
in his transparent dress.
I bend and stare at the hills
of his marble buttocks,
and see no dangle
of testicle or prick.
The man holds a baby,
neutered, too,

Bolero

with the face of a man,
wrinkled as a sundried tomato.

I see the clumsy seams
where granite shoulders
fit to glass arms,
porcelain clavicles
to wooden chests.
I wish I had a photograph
of me, a baby with a man's face
in my parent's arms.
I would keep it in my wallet
and look at it
when I needed to.

On the plaquette
I read the artist
considers her man and child
"tormented little figures."
She says she would not
have made them
that way
if she thought it was easy
to be a human being.

Where the Long Grass Bends

A gaggle of children
surround me.
They look at the statue
of the man and child.
The Brooklyn accent
of the tour guide
makes me lonely.
I like English accented
with the familiarity
of another tongue.
The guide tells the children
"Police have devices,
small metal ones
with antennae to find all the bombs."
The children look worried
until a small one shouts
"Gosh, look at the ceiling!"

It is vaulted and gold.

I think of Topkapi Palace
and the splendour
of invisibility.
I imagine a clan of people
with blue and brown,

unfragile, glass arms.
They can lift heavy things,
like people
and buildings.

In the museum bathroom,
in the water-spattered mirror
that reflects everyone as a bust,
I see my face.
I hear the drip of toilets
and am startled by my beauty.

Felix Dreams of the Dead

Rows of child-sized coffins: lidded, black, with varnished piano-skin. A silver tablet nailed to the first box reads:

Here lies Oboe who had a range from B-flat below middle C to the third G above middle C, the highest and chief member of the double-reed instruments. 1932–1946.

Only fourteen years old, Felix sighs (the war, the war) and opens the coffin. He touches the black flare at the oboe's base.

Inside the next coffin, Felix finds a honey-colored violin. A tag hangs from the lower right peg:

A Gagliano, with four strings tuned at intervals of a fifth

and a range from G below middle C to the fourth C above.
1884–1926.

The bow is warped and crisscrossed with termite passageways.

Atop the next coffin sits Ilona. Her boots are covered with sheep manure. She points to a plaque:

Here lies French Horn, who roused hunters but was mutilated in Leeds by a rabid hound. This brass instrument had a range in pitch of more than three octaves upward from two octaves below middle C. 1799–1820.

Conduct my heart, Ilona says and pulls Felix's head to her chest. Show me the shape of my tempo.

Closing his eyes, Felix listens.

It is the pattern of a two-beat *legato* (he pauses), and after a measure, it turns to a four-beat staccato. In the air, he sketches a triangle with a long, horizontal tail.

It looks like a torn kite, she says.

Yes. Can they be saved?

Lay your hands on them and they will live. She sounds like a clarinet; her words rise in a disciplined scale.

Felix walks toward a pear tree. The procession of caskets decrease in size. He looks at a miniature coffin, made for a fairy, he thinks, squinting to read the plaque. The words make him weep:

Bolero

Here lies Piccolo, small and shrill, pitched an octave above Flute.
1929–1975.

Under the pear tree, Felix finds his grandfather in a pine casket, a heap of chipped piano keys next to him. He claps his hands over his mouth. Remembering Ilona's instructions (Lay your hands on them) he leans down and touches his grandfather's cheek. He picks up the keys and hurls them against the pear tree. He hears a trill, ending in a chord: C major.

Over here! Felix calls. Come and play them! Come and make them live!

He leans against a coffin with the epitaph:

Here lies Cymbal, who lost his twin and died of grief:
1962–2001.

The room is filled with people, strangers to Felix. He watches them open coffins and lift the dead instruments. Some they put to their mouths, some they cradle, some they prepare to pluck. Suddenly, a high C from little piccolo. A low G from a cello played by a boy astride a casket. A blast from a crooked bassoon.

Resurrected! Felix cries.

At a one-legged piano, he finds Ilona: she bears no instrument.

You don't fool me, he tells her. I know where you hide it.

She taps her throat.

Play it for me, will you?

Opening her mouth, she drops her chin and narrows her lips into an oval. She sings: lone notes, bouncy, the veins in her neck strain, her stomach rounds and relaxes. Gradually, she warbles into *sotto voce* and Felix hears the other instruments bawling, a gruesome din of moldy wood, dented metal, and moth-eaten horsehair. Beneath the clamor, he discerns a melodic line. It is off-key, but he recognizes it.

The
Pelvis
Series

I.

Eve's father swung her onto his shoulders and gave her a ride to the indoor forest. She pinched his ears. She was farseeing: a giraffe.

"Duck," her father said as they passed through a door hanging with vines.

A white, plastic sky arched above. She heard a trickle of water, distant screeches of birds. She grabbed a hunk of her father's hair and gently kicked him; he lowered her to the ground.

At a fork in the path, they peered through the simulated fog seeping rhythmically from vents. Set back against the plastic horizon, between the trees, a small door framed a patch of real sky. Moisture dripped from the ceiling.

Her father raised a hand, cupped his ear. She heard crickets chirping; she nodded. To the left, watching them through a glass wall, was a chimpanzee.

Eve and her father walked down the Ape Path. The chimp kept pace, his brackish eyes inscrutable, his thick lashes feminine and curious. Eve watched the chimp, close enough to touch, to understand. She squeaked her fingers along the glass. In the dense foggy air, she knew the chimp by his steps, his eyes; she knew her father by his neck, the wedge of his back. Her tongue was flat in her mouth: blank, unnecessary.

When the path veered away from the glass enclosure, the chimp disappeared from her view. She yanked on her father's hand, and he lifted her to his shoulders.

II.

On a dig in South Africa (fieldwork for her linguistics doctorate), Eve unearthed a chimpanzee. It was 3.5 million years dead. She gazed into the empty eye sockets and beige muzzle of the intact skull. An hour later, she found shards of spine.

She worked on the computer, reconstructing the

placement of the chimpanzee's larynx. The partially reassembled skeleton lay on a table covered with black velvet, a cushion and contrasting background for the bones. With the help of the resident biologist—a timorous man with clumps of red back hair welling above his collar—Eve deduced the larynx to be high in the throat, restricting the range of sound.

She massaged her own larynx, low, like all *Homo sapiens*. She hummed a high note and made a cage of her fingers around the vibration.

That night, Eve got drunk. Three beers for each member of the American team and four each for the Africans because they haggled better, with charm. The hairy biologist produced a bottle of tequila and the Africans clapped and shouted for Eve as she tossed back five shots in five minutes. "You look like Ghana woman," one man said, and touched her helixed hair. "Where are your people from?"

"Could be Ghana. Could be anywhere," she said.

A game of charades was organized by the paleontologists who insisted on dividing: one team named Leakey, one, Johanssen. Eve sat next to the biologist and his tequila. When the Leakey group said that sound in charades was as legitimate as Piltdown Man, the game turned into a fight.

Eve leaned into the biologist: "So, Red, do you feed that animal on your back, or what? We all want to know."

He laughed and pulled a comb from his pocket. "Want to give it a whirl?" he asked, and rapped the comb sharply against her forehead.

"Not here," she said and staggered from the lab.

In the dark, on a mound of mistakenly excavated twentieth-century rabbit, lion, and hyena bones, Eve sat with her legs sprawled in front of her. The titanic sky rolled down to the earth in every direction, so that Eve stared straight ahead and still looked into the black star-crowded night, a piece of velvet studded with white bones. The biologist tapped her shoulder, and she leaned her head back.

"Gimme that comb," she said, "and take off that dirty shirt." A primitive fear, of decay, of the unknown, taunted her from the tar-pit sky. She knew it was eternal and complete. She was fragile, an inevitable fossil. The biologist removed his shirt.

Eve looked at him, at his red fringed pelt and triangular head. Against the night, his silhouette rose pointed and stout, blotting stars. She felt safe; his shape, like a tent, spoke of community. Reaching up, she pulled him onto the pile of bones. "They're sharp," he complained, and shrank from the triumph in her voice when she said, "I don't feel anything," and closed her eyes against the sky and the words and the unknown.

The biologist sat meekly, allowing her to tug at his red

back hair, wincing when she untangled a snarl. "It's nice," she whispered to him, her legs clamped around his pale fleecy waist, her fingers wielding the comb like a crude weapon.

III.

For her dissertation research, Eve took a job in Texas working with language-impaired children. One of her cases could not speak; eight-year-old Jamie vocalized and gestured, but was usually unable to make herself understood. During her frequent tantrums, she wrapped her hands with her blonde, waist-length hair and punched her mother mechanically.

No matter how her mother tied Jamie's hair, the child shook it loose. When she began yanking it out in fits of frustration, her mother cut it into a bob that curved around Jamie's face in shaggy points. With her short hair, Jamie was unwilling to punch, so she created a new expression of anger. By pointing at the fridge she demanded a juice box and then emptied it in one crushing squeeze, one livid slurp. She tossed the flattened juice box to the floor, then pounced on it and tore it to shreds with her hands and teeth, saving the mutilated plastic straws as trophies. If seriously confounded, she pulled out her own eyebrows and eyelashes and would not allow her mother to attach fake ones. Both speech therapy and sign language failed to help Jaime.

Eve investigated alternate methods. She read about a pygmy chimpanzee, or bonobo, named Kanzi, who learned to communicate through a system of lexigrams, a language called Yerkish.

The system pleased Eve: a computerized board covered with arbitrary symbols, each one representing a word: noun, adjective, or verb in the shape of a spiral, square, semicircle, rod. She saw possibilities: *I want pasta, I miss you, I'm tired.* A total of seven hundred potential words lined the lexigram board. The center performing the chimpanzee research also sponsored a program for speech-impaired children.

Eve wrote letters, e-mailed, telephoned the center, bombarding anyone who would listen with her credentials and interests. She said she would move to Georgia and agreed to learn the lexigram process first with chimpanzees, then humans, as the center requested.

She was granted a three-year internship (with no pay). She promised Jamie and her mother that she would send for them as soon as she began work with children.

IV.

When they met, Lola grabbed Eve's hand and brought her to the TV. They spent the afternoon watching a *Discovery* program on the migration patterns of monarch butterflies. Lola was a bonobo, with immense gaps between her teeth and hands textured like olive meat. She was fond of placing towels on her head; when she pulled the ends around her face, she looked uncommonly like Mother Theresa, benevolent and wise. In sunlight, red highlights streaked her long, black fur. Her ears wiggled when it thundered. She laughed easily, explosive, sounding like seagulls cavorting around a Dumpster. Because of a mild case of arthritis, she was not very dexterous, even clumsy when climbing. The red of her lips bled almost up to her nostrils, and a deep cove of wrinkled forehead interrupted her soft hair. If embarrassed, she covered her face with her hands.

"Lola, Lo-lo-lo-lo, Lola," Eve sang to her.

What amazed Eve most was the level of comprehension she read in Lola's eyes. She showed her pictures of Jamie, her own parents, her cat. She learned that Lola was pregnant and that her mother had died when she was eight. When Eve was twenty-four, her parents died in an airplane crash. As soon as she told Lola, she found herself clasped in a vigorous embrace.

Where the Long Grass Bends

The pregnancy was Lola's third; all her babies had been stillborn. Lola told Eve this using the lexigrams to say, "My babies quiet." She also told Eve she liked bananas and oranges and disliked the woman with white hair who mopped the floors ("Dirty White Head"), and she hid Eve's car keys at the end of each day—always in a different spot. Arriving home, Eve worked on her dissertation and wrote letters to Jamie and her mother. She sent them pictures of Lola playing dress-up and drinking vodka and cranberry juice with the American Sign Language chimps: Fouts, Jane, and Darwin. From the ASL chimps Lola learned the hand-signs for "Gimme," "More," and "Hurry," which she eventually combined into a sentence, "Hurry, Gimme More." In turn, she taught her friends the lexigrams for "Lola Pretty" and "Please Hug."

Hats and scarves and accessories of any kind thrilled Lola. She loved to try on clothes and look in the mirror; sometimes her hands flew to her face in embarrassment, sometimes her smile stretched happy and gapped. She had a collection of postcards, reproduced prints by Frida Kahlo (her favorite: *Diego on my Mind*) and Georgia O'Keeffe (she ignored the flower paintings but was fascinated by the bone and sky pieces). She played darts—the bullseye a photograph of Noam Chomsky. She adored UPS deliverers; ripping open packages was one of her assigned chores. She danced to polka music, L. L. Cool J. But only one activity, car rides, evoked cheers of delight. When Eve told her they were going for a drive, Lola wrapped an orange silk scarf around her head, Grace Kelly style. She took her backpack and stuffed it full of bananas, audiotapes, magazines (she demanded *Playgirl* whenever she was in estrus or if she had just encountered her favorite man, a grad student with green eyes who was studying bisexuality and face-to-face copulation in bonobos). Beethoven remained her favorite composer, from childhood through adulthood, particularly the Seventh Symphony conducted by Herbert von Karajan. Once she and Eve turned onto the open road, Lola put Beethoven in the deck, rolled down her window, and stuck out her hand, tapping against the side of the car and causing many near accidents. She had a hatred for policemen on motorcycles, especially if they wore sunglasses, and Eve always had to speed in case Lola tried to unseat a cop with her long arms.

In winter, Lola pouted. Forced to stay indoors, she used the lexigram board to sign "Bad oranges," and "Dirty Eve take Good Lola outside." The year Eve came to the language center, the winter was unusually long. Mid-April, the first warm day, Lola followed Eve around, sensing a treat. "Yes, Lola," Eve told her. "We're going for a car ride."

Lola donned her maternity tank top, her gravid

stomach bulging, her baby due in two months. She waddled around, fanning herself with the portable lexigram sheet as Eve packed a picnic basket with grapes, cheese sandwiches, a jar of pickles, and napkins. She stowed the basket in the trunk of the car.

With all the windows rolled down, orange scarf wrapped around her head, and wind rippling her sleek, conditioned fur, Lola waved at houses and children looking out the back of a school bus. She whipped her face into a frenzy of terrifying expressions, the children laughing encouragement and forcing their arms joyfully out the side-windows to give her the finger. She gave it back. The wind inflated her orange scarf and she broke the sideview mirror trying to look inside her mouth.

When they stopped at a gas station, the attendant ran from Lola, who got out of the car and stood on one leg, stretching the other above her head. He locked himself in the booth and stared at Lola's pendulous breasts, full stomach, and red engorged sex. Since Lola was always allowed to pay for gas, Eve handed her a ten dollar bill and told her to slide it gently under the slot. The attendant whimpered and cried as Lola gave him the money, grunting her friendly grunt.

As they neared the park, Lola became pensive and quiet. Usually when Eve asked her what she was thinking about, Lola ignored her. Eve reached out and touched

Lola's head. She asked, "What are you thinking about?" Lola poked at the lexigram "Mommy."

"Are you thinking of your Mommy?" asked Eve. "Wuhh, wuh, wuh," Lola replied in her guttural voice, and twisted her toes. Eve patted Lola's stomach, sagging under the bottom of the tank top. Tilting the lexigram board, she tapped "Mommy," then patted Lola's stomach again and wondered if she herself would ever be a mother. At thirty-eight, three years younger than Lola, she did not feel ready for children.

"Tell me, Lola, what's in your stomach?" Eve asked, and Lola pointed triumphantly to the symbol, "Baby." They turned into the park.

Black fur gleaming red, Lola led the way to a path they had used once in the fall, peeled off her tank top and unwound the orange scarf from her head. She hardly walked bipedally now, preferring the protective four-hand stance, her back shielding the life inside her. The woods smelled faintly of scallions. Lola gathered sorrel for Eve and daffodils for herself, some of which she ate. Nostrils flared, she loped ahead, scouting. When the sun drifted behind clouds, the air turned cool. Eve mimicked thrush and sparrow calls, trying to engage the birds in conversation. Lola swatted at mosquitoes and ate the ones she caught. "Good protein," Eve told her.

Where the Long Grass Bends

On the bank of a small creek, they spread out a blanket and unpacked the picnic basket. A crow circled above them and called out, the sound echoing. The crow chased its own voice, spinning in wide, flirtatious circles. "Too bad humans understand echoes," Eve said to Lola. "We could have been spared some loneliness." She folded the paper napkins into triangles.

Once Lola gave birth, the center would concentrate on teaching her baby and monitoring how much he learned from his mother (they already knew it was a boy, but did not tell Lola). When the baby turned three, Lola would stop working altogether—money at the center had to be reserved for learning chimps and post-retirement upkeep was expensive. The center tried to accrue money to study old age in chimpanzees, but no donors were interested, and Lola would be sent to a conservancy with other retired chimps and bonobos, a better fate than the last set of aged ASL chimps who had been shipped to a research institute and injected with hepatitis.

Eve wondered if she would be friends with Lola's son as she watched her trying to open the jar of pickles, grunting in frustration. Holding the jar out to Eve, Lola mimed a twisting motion with her right hand and furrowed her brow pleadingly.

They ate the entire jar of pickles, Lola teaching Eve

how to eat with her toes. When they finished eating, they lay on their sides and flipped through magazines. It began to rain. Plashes of water fell onto the magazines, sticking the pages together. Out of the blanket, they made a roof and huddled together.

V.

Lola retired at forty-five, Jamie's second year in the children's program, and the year Eve finished her dissertation and was hired as a permanent member of the center. It was Eve who arranged for Lola's send-off picnic at her favorite park. Numerous guest speakers signed up for the event: a specialist on hominid teeth Eve knew from her days on the dig, an ethologist, a cultural anthropolgist. Eve had ordered round tables, white tablecloths, and peach napkins folded into swans (in honor of chimpanzee Washoe and her creation of WATER BIRD) for the wealthy sponsors' table and Lola's center table where Pan—Lola's three-year-old son—Eve, Fouts, Jane, and Darwin also sat. Green and white balloons tossed above the back of each chair. Eve was wearing a new spring dress, white and sheer, flecked with little pink roses. She had twisted her hair and forced earrings through her long-closed piercings.

Lola jabbered to Pan and fed him carrots. She tried to

rub up against a handsome paleontologist from Kenya. A few children chased stray programs skipping across the lawn. Eve's group of speech-impaired children sat at the next table, Jamie happily among them. The child's hair was long again, almost to her waist. She sat on her mother's lap and used a lexigram board to demand more coleslaw. After only three months in the program, Jamie had begun to communicate. Lately, she combined sign language with lexigrams. Sometimes she said "Mommy" or "Eve" in a whisper. She and Lola wore the same pink party hat.

The paleontologist from Kenya gave Lola a plastic model of a human pelvis. She sniffed it lovingly and toyed with herself. One speaker remained: Eve. After her introduction, she walked up to the podium and stood under an oversized green umbrella stamped with white chimpanzees. She tapped the microphone, unexpectedly nervous. She saw Lola lying on her back with Pan balanced on her hands and feet, playing airplane. Pan giggled, sounding like a small seagull. His fur glowed with a red hue.

Eve talked about Lola and her accomplishments as a student and mother, her generosity, her love of paintings, dogs, Mississippi John Hurt, her long sentences. She told the story of Roger Fouts and Washoe, the ASL chimp, and the day a deaf girl came to the house to visit. Sitting in the kitchen, the child saw Washoe through the window, and at the same time that she signed "MONKEY" to Washoe, Washoe signed "BABY" to the child. Human-raised and cross-fostered, Washoe thought of herself as a *Homo sapiens*. The first time she met other chimpanzees she disdainfully referred to them as "Black Bugs," but after a few days she called them "Man" or "Woman," deciding they were all one people, all primates.

VI.

The picnic was over. Stars crammed the sky; the moon was a tilted crescent. Lola had consumed three pounds of grapes and seven chili dogs. Pan was frisky from too much iced tea. Eve supervised the removal of tables and chairs, and made sure the microphone was returned to the soundman. She took out her earrings and put them in her backpack. She was tired.

At ten, the lights in the park went out. Eve, Lola, and Pan ambled to the van together. The crickets buzzed like power tools: screwguns, circ saws, drills. Lola carried the plastic pelvis and led the way through the woods. She knew where the van was parked. Eve always forgot.

When they came out of the trees and onto the blacktop, they stopped and looked at the sky. The stars pulsed and blazed; the Milky Way cloudy, like the wax on a plum.

"Orion," Eve said. "And look! There are the Pleiades."

Lola waved the pelvis. She stood bipedally, and so did Pan. Silently, they gazed up. The crickets buzzed and clicked. A thin cloud sidled in front of the moon. Eve stared at the stars, searching for a pattern.

She asked Lola for the pelvis. She looked at the sky through the hip sockets so the stars were framed in white circles of bone. On the back of Lola's "Pelvis With Moon" postcard she had read that Georgia O'Keeffe held flowers and bones against the sky to see the objects clearly, to get a sense of foreground and distance.

She pulled her eye farther away from the hip socket: the curve of white bone; the black sky pitted with light.

"Pelvis With Stars," she said to Lola, and gave the bone back to her. "Like your painting. You know the one?"

Lola held the bone up to her own eyes and hooted. She signed "SKY" to Pan, who copied the gesture, sweeping the air with his hand. He begged for the pelvis in high, pleading grunts.

"Good. Yes. Sky," Eve said to Pan, making the motion herself.

Lola watched Pan's hand, then grabbed his thumb and moved it away from his fingers.

"It was a bit slurred," Eve agreed.

Pan tried again, his hand in front of his face, the arc smooth, expansive. He kept his eyes on his mother: "SKY."

Lola chuffed and gave him the pelvis.

"That's right," Eve said, looking up. "Sky."

An
Outline
of No
Direction

I. North

   A. If I were a ship, I would be listing.

      1. A road map of America, next to me, belted into the passenger seat. It is sprawling, officious and coffee-stained: spangled with lakes; mountain ranges like zippers. My two-dimensional companion who tries to escape when I roll down the windows.

         a. What would I do if I lost you?
            1. Wander.

         b. But I prefer the fraudulence of consulting you, as if I have intentions, as if distance and destination factor into my plan. The

achievement of reaching the city, crossing
the river, connecting to the interstate that I
have marked, in pen (hyacinth purple).

c. I fold you against your inclinations. And
   when you have settled into the new creases, I
   fold you again and again, until you are
   pliable, velour, and reformed.

d. Yellow kamikaze moths plastered to the
   windshield make it difficult to see, to
   navigate.

   1. But are they flying into me? Or am I
      driving into them? Who is to blame for
      this loss of life, these killings?

B. Today, I feel Northern.

   1. North: it glitters. Twinkly, pure, bracing. Cold
      preserves; cold exterminates. Cold invites
      protection: mittens, hats, scarves, boots,
      thermals, cabled sweaters, fleece pants, goggles,
      muffs, masks. We are safe. We are covered. We
      are layered. We have every reason to stay in bed
      under goosedown and wool, every reason to inch
      closer to the fire, every reason to curl around the
      person beside us. It is cold. Leave us alone.

   2. If I head due North, I will drive through
      piousness, prudery, and of course, snow.

An Outline of No Direction

Clapboard houses, ivy, erratic lane-changers, white-washed steeples, salt trucks. How much of this is stereotype?

   a. Right now, I feel you wedged deep inside my chest.

   b. At noon, I felt your restlessness.

   c. At three, you were asleep, fetal and happy.

      1. If you think I am trying to get away from you, you may be right.

      2. If only you had asked me to stay.

C. I am running out of money, my stomach is shrinking, my teeth are stuck with sunflower shells and apple peels. In the next town, I will stop at the third Friendly's I see, and ask, Do you need any help?

   1. I have experience. I can serve and balance plates, fill ramekins, shine knives, funnel ketchup, and smile.

      a. They are not hiring. I will eat another apple.

D. Crossing the Mackinaw Bridge in fog I follow the fevered taillights of the truck in front of me. If it drives off through the steel girders and plunges, far far down into the slate water, so will I.

   1. Gratitude, as we glide safely back onto land, this truck and I. Passing on the left, I look at its

mudflaps, wider than my car, and see the
forearm of the driver leaning on the steering
wheel. We obey the lines: white, yellow, dotted,
and unbroken. We know what is expected of us.

E. At Sault Sainte-Marie I come to a border crossing.
I pull up to a square metal hut, a green light
blinking above it. The woman inside the hut
mistrusts me. I am dark, everywhere, dark, a
terrorist, a refugee.

1. Do you speak English?

a. Yes.

2. Identify yourself, she barks.

a. I gape. What a question, I say, and she repeats
it.

1. Well, I don't like red grapes—they leave
an aftertaste, like steam from an iron, that
I just can't abide.

3. Mam, she says, a clear threat, that three-letter
word, Identify yourself.

a. I gape. I can't, I say, miserably.

4. Step out of the car, mam, she says, Yes mam, I
say, and I stand in the freezing night, my breath,
a caul, as she paws through my backseat in
surgical gloves waving a high-powered flashlight
as bright as noon.

An Outline of No Direction

    a. There's nothing in here, she says, finally, disgusted.

        1. My possessions

          a. pennies

          b. three maps

          c. a toothbrush

          d. books

    5. Are you entering Canada on business or pleasure?

    6. Forget it, I say. I'm not entering at all.

F. I have never seen North Dakota by day, only at night, which is the best way to see the state.

    1. The Northern Lights: tremendous bands of green and yellow and white, carting, horizontally, across the sky.

    2. Shooting stars, comets, satellites, meteors, dazzle and streak, the wind lashes, the wind is fierce, I squat and urinate at the side of the road, the cattle crossings, innumerable, and I am always alone, alone and palely loitering, no matter how frequently I stop to buy jerky and hear my own voice say to a bleary girl behind a countertop littered with Lotto tickets: Cold, tonight, huh?

G. Carpe Diem.

    1. I told my mother, when I turned seven, that

this was my new motto. I thought she would be pleased—what could be more productive than the act of seizing the day? And how I wanted to seize that day, to wrestle, throttle, and consume it.

2. She regarded me with a mixture of
   a. horror
   b. suspicion
3. You'll never amount to anything if you go around seizing the day, she said. That's not how to get a pension or health insurance, she said.

H. I am taking myself to McDonald's.
1. In the lot, I park next to a car crammed full of children, a father, drowning in arms and legs and pigtails, in the driver's seat.
2. On line, the aroma of hash browns incites me to *tsk* and sigh at how slowly the visored and smocked move. I stand behind a woman who smells of alcohol swabs and baby powder.
   a. She shouts into a walkie-talkie.
      1. Lindsay, stop picking on your father. Maisie, don't just say soda, be specific, what kind? All right. OK, here we go, pay attention, all of you. I'll take eleven McMuffins, fourteen orange juices, seven

> Cokes, twenty hash browns, what Patrick? make that twenty-three, and two coffees.

2. The walkie-talkie crackles as she puts it in her pocket.

3. The voices of her children, mumbling from her hip.

I. Beneath the permafrost, the snow, there are dinosaurs, mammoths, Aleutians, gold. Up here, in the North, there are bridges of ice, melting, there are bridges of land, emerging.

J. I see my breath, I am breathing, the evidence is unmistakable. No need for mirrors here, life is apparent, life is visible; it smells of gingivitis and impending root canals.

II. West

    A. Time zones slide by, but I do not notice. I meet a Mennonite woman at a KOA site who trades with me: a book for a bonnet.

        1. I am a pioneer.

        2. Tonight, she will dream of Uriah Heep, moving like grease across a hot pan.

            a. A fair trade. Westward, ho. Further up and further in. Onward and upward.

    B. For dinner I eat freshly-stolen corn, roasted over a

small fire. I squeeze lime juice into the runnels between the carbon-scarred kernels. At the next gas station, I lock myself in the bathroom with a bar of soap and wash my pits at the sink.

1. A truck-stop shower is no place for a woman, although it is a good place to eat blueberry pie in peace.

2. A delivery man, wrangling cases of Pepsi, watches me pour a can of Coke down my throat. That stuff'll give you a rash, he says.

   a. America's age-old battles.

C. Into the North Cheyenne Reservation, I drive by a puberty rite, a boy in a T-shirt yellow as corn, running. Instead of being followed by men on horseback, he is followed by men in eroded pickup trucks. A big-dropped sun-shower spatters around him.

1. The bunched clouds, gauzy light: ceiling, unlimited. A man is born.

2. My fan belt snaps. An old woman in orthopedic shoes replaces it for me, free of charge, behind her mobile home. I watch *Jeopardy* and *Wheel of Fortune* on a black-and-white TV. Uncolored, Pat Sajack is less acidic, Alex Trebek, less forlorn.

An Outline of No Direction

  D. I am enamored with I-90 and Route 212.
1. Dear so-and-so: I won't be returning.
2. The road is my lover, the road, the road.
3. Driving West, into the setting sun, is like dying: serene, glorious, and awed.

  E. I pass a blonde boy pulling a blonde girl in a red wagon along the side of the highway.

  F. West: dream, stagger, elevate. Unfenced, unbridled, 1% humidity, the way of legend, of hope, long, straight roads and undefined speed limits, black Angus cows and soaring hills, the wells, dry, my heart, wet; there are no steeples, only clouds and haystacks.

  G. I buy an avocado and the girl at the cash register says, I didn't even know we sold artichokes. She suggests I purchase some sunscreen. For that skin, she says. I have no idea what she's talking about.

  H. At a SandwichHaus, I ask for a salad and am served a burger on a lone leaf of iceberg lettuce.

  I. I am hungrier than ever.

  J. Wherever I am, I am drawn North or West. It is a compulsion.

  K. When I reach Montana, I will stop driving. I need an edge, a space of Westness unexplored, undiscovered, by me. I will stop here, in Montana,

and think of that Westness, expectant and
promising, for the future.

L. I remember, I remember, my parents, raking
   leaves. The West is where all such memories go,
   the ones that brim and burn under the
   concentrated glare of a magnifying glass.

III. South

A. I am afraid. It is irrational, but gripping.

   1. In a store, in South Carolina, I see a light
      brown child with a white mother, black father.
      The store owner looks from the mother to the
      father and then to the child and says:

      a. That's disgusting.
      b. The child becomes an article, a that, the
         equivalent of a dish towel, a telephone, a
         lawn mower.
      c. The parents, an aberration.
      d. He showed them a shotgun and they left
         his place of business. I followed them out
         the door, hiding my own light brown face
         in my hands.

B. Awakening in a motel with a turquoise swimming
   pool, I am confused. The air conditioning is
   vigorous, frigid. It is winter, I think, and I am in

the North. Outside, a child splashes in the pool. The palms bend; a dog licks runny eggs from a plate.

C. Kindness is a choice.

D. In Tennessee, I was pulled over for driving too slowly and brought to a police station to fill out some forms. A woman in an orange swing coat came in holding a plastic recorder in one hand and her child's fist in the other. She told a policeman:

   1. My Charles stole this recorder from preschool.

      a. She held the instrument out in front of her, like a relic.

   2. He turned four years old today and stole a recorder. Not only did he steal this recorder, but he hid it under the sofa. Not only did he try and conceal his DECEIT, but he concealed it badly, left a corner of it sticking out. I asked him maybe you were just beggin' to be caught? Maybe your soul was heavy with your bad deed? And when I asked Charles why he stole the recorder when he knows his Mama would buy him one if he asked, he said, "I dunno." Child can't even give me a decent excuse for his deviant behavior. So I told Charles that

even though I'm his mother and we've got
nobody in the world but each other, I'd have to
turn him in because Stealing Is Wrong and I
don't want a bad boy living with me. Had one
already, if you know what I'm sayin', and that
was enough. So here he is, officer. I'm gonna
leave it up to you and the justice system
whether or not he should stay in jail. Maybe on
account of his youth, you could just give him a
good talking to and if it ever happens again,
then lock him up for good. Whatever you see
fit is fine with me. I just want to do the right
thing. I want Charles here to confess his crime
and apologize.

3. Charles was taken into a jail cell. The door,
   locked, behind him.

4. He sat on a cot next to a plastic toilet and
   pathetic sink and received a lecture On
   Stealing.

   a. I'm sorry, he wailed, tears worming down his
      muddy cheeks.

5. When he was released from the cell, his
   mother squeezed his hand and told him all was
   forgiven (he said, Thank you, Jesus) and she
   hoped he would not disappoint her in this

manner again. She thanked the police officers (duly impressed) and then she and Charles left.

6. I signed my name four times on four different forms and then I, too, left.

7. Morality is also a choice.

    a. Do not frighten me with devils and brimstone. I am not a child. Show me consequences. Show me your discontent. That is more effective than a promise of doomed afterlife or a belt strap.

    b. Charles never stole again.

E. South: swoony, secretive, callused, slow. Pitchfork, noose, bandy legs, gospel. A woman with blue, leaf-shaped eyes, a mind, a heart, like a chain saw. I see her as a slot into which all things good fit. The South is redeemed, for she exists down there. It is not all terrifying. It is not all hate, mulled in drawls, polite chitchat, and eyelet parasols.

1. In the North, the Mississippi is a trickle, barely in need of a bridge.

2. In the South, I ride a roller coaster over Dolly Parton's bosom; I scream in terror, in admiration, zooming through her cleavage. I see, through glass, a sparkling cape, a fried

peanut butter and banana sandwich. I see
Elvis, standing alone. I go to a mission church
and eat *arroz y frijoles*. I take a steam
locomotive, pitch-black, wide-skirted, to an old
silver town and buy a fork. I see a black woman
in rags holding a white baby in silk. I see a
black man napping in the shade, a hand resting
in his upturned hat.

IV. East

  A. Home

    1. New York, I will be my own census. I will stand
      on one of your street corners and count the
      people going by. Some will smile,
      understanding what I am doing and why it
      satisfies. One Korean, One Palestinian, One
      Nigerian, One Pakistani, One Crow, One half
      Puerto Rican, One half Iranian, One Cuban,
      One Italian, One Brazilian, One Mexican:
      Seven Women, Four Men, Ten Homosexuals,
      Five Biracials, One Transgender, One
      Schizophrenic, Two Catholics, One Buddhist,
      One Jew, Two Hindus, Two Muslims, Three
      Seventh-Day Adventists, Eight Diabetics, One
      Paraplegic, Three Exiles, Five Homeless.

An Outline of No Direction

B. Driving east, into the sunrise, it is wonderful to see these beginnings, every day, remarkable.

    1. Dear so-and-so: I am coming home. To you.

C. If you continue to drive east straight through the Holland Tunnel, you will come out the other side, I promise. Times Square, so bright, you will think it is the sun in your eyes (the work of electricians, the genius of wires and cables). Buildings, dimpled with light, the air, laced with languages, your mouth full of international food. Ah, happiness.

D. The East is a portal. We are all yearning to be free, but it is crowded here and the grass near the Esplanade has been flattened by our rear ends.

    1. Next summer, we can sit on it. Until then, it must rest, regenerate.

    2. I will watch Diana Ross rollerblade. I will march for gay pride and wear a black Barbie on my head at Wigstock. I, a fruit fly, will cruise up and down the Hudson, the piers, with the other boys. We will be attracted by purple spandex; we will lick our lips, and if you get in our way we will call you Bitch.

E. East: Long Island with your kosher delis and sumps and strip malls.

Where the Long Grass Bends

1. A girl, leaning into the candled cake that marked the passage of her thirteen years, I saw her brown ringlets, armored in hairspray, go up in flames.
2. I watched lacrosse games and loved a boy who smelled of soap, clean and good.
3. I dove for colored rings in Allyson's pool.
    a. From the bottom, we saw the sky distorted; we shaved her brother's toe hairs, dipping razors in tupperware bowls filled with steaming water and floating with bergs of Barbasol.
4. Through photographs of cats, local fires, the Sound, pinned to a clothesline, I ran with my first friend. I prowled and scratched tree-bark, sniffing (hard) for the scent of rootbeer. I was afraid of the Pink Floyd poster. I liked Toad, tea with milk. I liked the violin and the way she played it, tenderly.

V. The Stone Collector
   A. In my backyard, I make America. I find stones at the beach, in the shape of states. They are not to scale.
      1. Texas is very small.
      2. Delaware, a boulder.

B. At the beach I look up and see color: fluorescent pink, the shade of a lawn flamingo. Sprayed across the sky, a stunning display. Spray-painted on an aluminum bird: sad.

C. The stones toss in the waves and wash onto shore, the stones are buried, the stones are stamped with ferns, the stones are arrowheads of Kickapoo, Seneca.

D. I name you Kentucky, I name you Idaho, I name you Arizona, I name you Minnesota, I name you Maine. Pressing you into the grass, your borders do not match up, you are irregular, you are America. In a wheelbarrow, I bring sticks and pile them on your western and eastern shores, New York, California, I pile them at the tip of Florida and the base of New Mexico, I bring these sticks, these immigrants, these emulsifiers. Let them in, I holler, and pile them up and up until they are as tall and unsteady as a bonfire.

   1. I keep the garden hose close by to thwart and dampen pyromaniacs.

E. A scoop of pebbles for Hawaii; a slab of obsidian, smaller than Rhode Island but correctly shaped is Alaska.

F. I stand, with one foot in Pennsylvania, one foot in

Iowa, straddling the Midwest, like Blue Earth's
Jolly Green Giant.

    1. The Philippines: gravel by the mailbox. Puerto
       Rico: a sliver of granite under the barbecue.

G. My mother and I, we take the Staten Island Ferry
   and smile when the boat tilts. We laugh at the
   seagulls flying alongside the railing; we feel the
   wind and think of a red-haired man and his black-
   haired bride, and why they are gone, and how it is
   lonely without them. The nuns, my mother says
   suddenly, they taught us that water is blue. I always
   said, It's green (they pulled my hair). I'm glad to
   see it's still green, she says and smiles.

    1. To me the water looks blue. But I am glad my
       mother sees green where I see blue.

H. My father and I, we drive under a dinner-plate
   moon, listening to Concerto 5: *Emperor.*
   Whistling, we are indistinguishable from the other.
   We think of America and the feel of her when she
   is a stranger and when she is home. We drive
   though fir trees and over railroad tracks. We are
   hungry and hope the *kachori* is fresh, and the
   restaurants in Jackson Heights open, despite the
   late hour.

Blue,
Without
Sorrow

*L*over, where are you? Fish. Flesh. Flame. I am waiting for you.

Do you remember, Roderigo, the game we played? On the floor of Mama's closet, we chanted *patience patience patience*. We sat in silence, waiting, the softness of Mama's dresses against our faces, the acrid, animal scent of her shoes in the air. Light seeped under the closet door. You did not see it, Roderigo, but it surrounded you all the same.

You burst from the closet first and I followed, having won. I chased you to the barn, running circles around the stored peanuts, Daddy's new crop. We rolled over the burlap bags stamped, MEXICO: CACAHUETES, up and up the piles of nuts till we reached the summit and sank into the heap.

Where the Long Grass Bends

When we washed our hands before dinner, our fingers met in the gush of pump water and I remembered the closet, the shoes, dim and specklike, pushed back by the feel of my body rolling over peanuts, shucking the red-brown skins, the splinter and crunch interrupted by Mama's call to food.

Come for me, collect me, why do you torment me?

I was ten years old the day Roderigo and I snuck away from Daddy to throw stones in the pond. We squatted on our haunches, picking out pebbles and arcing them into the water. A large red, green, and gold fish, as big as our goat, leaped out of the pond, water fanning around it like wings. The fish was not really coming toward us both. Roderigo's sloped nose descended in fear; he knew it only wanted me, only want me, no one else. You. You touched me on the chin with your red flopping mouth then recoiled, backward, entering the pond tail-first. No splash, no ripple, as if you had never existed.

At home, Roderigo told Daddy about the fish, about You. The feeling of your wet mouth on my chin, the curve of your glorious, book-sized scales, like a rush of cold water over me. I felt Daddy turn to question me, but I could not see, speak, move. He and Roderigo, I felt them faintly, but the wind of you blowing around me was strong. They carried me to a bed where I lay flattened by the weight of you: rapt.

Blue, Without Sorrow

I remained that way for three months. Later, Roderigo told me that Daddy built my coffin in the barn among the peanuts. By the pond, near the gopher holes, he and the boys dug my grave and called the Padre in for Last Rites. I remember the idea of death beating around me, winged, and then I died, and I do not remember anything but the cracking and the crunching, the sound of a thousand peanuts, shelled. Roderigo said they wept over my small body when they heard my breathing stop. They wept for no one knows how long and then I opened my eyes and said, "It is true, the only way to see Him is to die." Then I began to scream, and the sound of my screams made the pigs scream in sympathy, it sounded so much like the slaughter of one of their brothers. When Daddy asked me what was the matter, I called out words: "Sick. Home. Homesick." I do not remember anything but the crunching and the cracking.

After that day, my family claimed there was no difference between my sounds of death and happiness. If I laughed, the pigs formed a circle, tails in, snouts out. My family feared the strength of my resolve and bragged to the Padre that I had willed myself dead. Daddy spent less time in the fields and more time praying.

The story reached Daddy by way of a newspaper that covered his lap as he sat in the barn, chickens pecking at his brown shoelaces. He read well enough to decipher the headline: *Virgin Mary Miracle.* "Teresa," he called. Roderigo and I were cleaning the stable; I leaned my rake against the door. "Teresa," he called again, "Come and practice your reading."

As I climbed onto his lap, he lifted the newspaper. Pointing under the headline, he said, "Start here," then spread the paper over me, a blanket. I liked the weight of it, and I read the first paragraph aloud: *During a mass at St. George's Church in Madaba, Jordan, an icon of the Virgin Mary suddenly grew a third, blue hand.*

"Stop there," Daddy said "I'm thinking."

He folded the paper; my knees were blackened from the print. "Back to the stable," he said, and I went.

That night, he and the Padre opened Mama's box of teaching supplies. They took out her globe and spun it—oceans scrolled by, Mexico, yellow and pink—until they found the tiny country of Jordan. Through a series of calculations performed with an almanac and the feather of our one black chicken, they determined that the appearance of the blue hand coincided with the moment of my death. They promised me to God in a pact that took place over warm bottles of beer. I, Teresa, was the child who would join the church. I was not consulted.

• • •

Blue, Without Sorrow

It was the tenth child, born dead, who killed our mother. I knew then I would not marry; she had been beautiful; we made her old, brittle. Digging for peanuts hardened my hands, digging in the wizened ground. I was happy with only the gophers for company.

I do not remember when I changed, but I am sure you do, Roderigo. I wore Mama's printed dresses, carried with her when she came to Mexico from New Orleans as a young teacher. I spent hours examining myself in her gilt mirror, smoothing makeup over my face. I felt I should be beautiful and wore the dresses and cosmetics to dig in the peanut fields; I asked Him to come see me. Tirelessly, I searched for him, throwing sand and clay, layers of the earth's lining behind me. My baskets overflowed with peanuts but still I could not find him. How he mocked me, left me, alone on the ground, surrounded by peanuts.

When I had used the last of Mama's makeup I could bear my loneliness and shame no longer. He would not come, no matter how I begged or groveled, no matter how beautiful I made myself. I felt he loved another; I felt his love faithless, and I ate a basket's worth of peanuts, ripping up the earth, crushing clods of dirt between my fingers and stuffing the nuts, some with shells, some skinless, into my mouth. With my hard hands, I dug a hole and stuck my head into it, smelling for peanuts, for Him, but still he did not save me from my degradation, Mama's dress blowing up to my shoulders, dirt filling my mouth. He would not come to me. I felt him nowhere.

I forgot him and found Manuel. I went back to *escuela* and found Manuel, an ugly, crooked boy, eight years my senior and still in school. One day he followed me home and told a story he thought would shock me, though it did not.

He said when he was born, his sister, Rosa, refused to look at him. His parents thought it was jealousy. After weeks of ignoring Manuel, Rosa finally said she would talk to the baby, but only if she could see him alone. The parents were reluctant—perhaps she wanted to harm her brother? They had heard of such things happening with cats. But they lay the baby on their bed and left the room. When Rosa shut the door, they leaned against the outside of it and listened. They heard her feet smacking against the floor, and her slight weight forcing a sigh from the bed as she sat. They heard baby Manuel squeak, and then they heard nothing and became afraid. Just as they were about to open the door, they heard Rosa say, soft and pleading, "Tell me about God; I am forgetting."

When we graduated, Manuel took me to the city on the back of his motorbike. The people exhausted me, the great ache drifting over them. They longed for something larger than themselves; I recognized the familiar scent.

Manuel and I stayed in the city for six months living in a small room across from the Palacio Nacional, rented to us by a muscular woman who wound bright, American stockings around her head. I sold postcards to tourists and believed in Manuel with a fervent devotion. But he, too, left me and refused to come when I called, busy with the landlady and the Mexican stockings on her legs. He said I made him feel false because he knew he did not deserve my ardor.

I took his motorbike. I found a dead dove on the steps of St. Francis, severed its head, and left it on the landlady's doormat. With my peanut-hardened hands, I wove a crown of thorns and tucked it under the sheets of Manuel's and my bed to prick their ugly feet when they slipped in together. Then I drove home to my family and drowned the motorbike in the pond. Purple thistles covered the mound of my old grave. The gopher holes were filled with rows of corn. Your sloped nose, Roderigo, no longer afraid, only sad. All but one of our brothers gone to America. Daddy was dead. And Rodergio, with bent back, worked to save our land and business. I, too, decided to go to America. Roderigo approved once our brothers returned, disgusted, saying it was a country for women.

Where the Long Grass Bends

I contacted my mother's family in Arizona; I would live with them and go to college. Before leaving, I knelt at Daddy's grave and vowed to honor his promise to God. A scrub jay watched me from the pepper tree. I said that one day I would join the church. As I said the words, I did not mean them, for in those days I had no love for God, but I thought it was what Daddy wanted to hear.

Then, you came. Uncalled, you. A reunion.

In my uncle's home, on Christmas Eve, I dreamed of a man with blue skin, the color of toothpaste, wearing a golden crown stabbed with peacock feathers. He took me from my bed and led me to the bathroom. He stopped up the sink and placed my hands under the running faucet. Red, green, and gold fish, small and bright as pennies, swam in the stream. When the water lapped the edges of the sink, the man took my face in his hands—his palms smelled of peanuts, his palms the soft blue of morning, his knuckles, navy and smooth. His eyes glittered like sequins, tender scales. When he pressed his mouth against my chin, I did not feel his lips, burning at the same temperature as my own.

I awakened in the bathroom, my hands pressed flat on the bottom of the dry sink, a ring shining red, gold, and green on my fourth finger. After the dream, for almost a

Blue, Without Sorrow

year, I was sick every morning. I suffered from not seeing Him. Sometimes, if I slept in the afternoon, I dreamt of the blue man, shirtless and eating a fish. He tipped back his head, the inside of his mouth, turquoise, his tongue, bright red. Tail-first, the fish disappeared down his lapis throat. I knew then I would fulfill Daddy's promise.

You courted me and I will have no other. You are mine, all mine. I am blue enough.

During college, I looked after the daughter of one of my professor's. All the money I earned was sent home to Roderigo. Our family land was cracking from drought, the peanuts shriveling in their hourglass coffins.

The professor and her husband worked late Monday through Wednesday. I read to their little girl and taught her to count to one hundred in Spanish. With our eyes closed, we played hide-and-seek on the open desert. *Noventa y ocho, noventa y nueve, cien.* The house was filled with books: *Woman the Hunter, The Golden Ass, The Demon King and the Virgin.* They were not kept on bookshelves but piled functionally, serving as tables, coat racks, hassocks. After I tucked the girl in to sleep, I had time for myself.

One Tuesday, I settled on the couch with an orange book. A book for children, consoling to me. It smelled of aching cities and was entitled: *Bride of God*. In disbelief, I read:

There was a woman named Mira and her faith was with God. Krishna, he is blue, he is God, he dances and wears peacock feathers in his crown.

I took out the sandwich my uncle had made for my dinner and reread the words:

peacock feathers in his crown.

As I unwrapped the sandwich, I saw a wrinkled face in the channels of the tinfoil, unrecognizable except for the color, blue. I understood how He hears us—not with the noise of words, but with the noise of longing. I read on:

Mira was a Rajput princess. As a child, she asked her mother, who will I marry? Her mother gave her a statue of Krishna, playing his flute. She said, "This is your husband." Mira washed her Lord's feet every night and kissed his neck when the sun rose.

When she turned sixteen, her father told her she was to marry to a Rajput prince. In her heart, Mira grieved; in her heart, she was already wed. But she married the prince, and they were happy together.

The prince's family worshipped the goddess Durga. They felt it inauspicious of Mira to praise Krishna. In an effort to

Blue, Without Sorrow

be rid of the girl, they told the prince she was unfaithful. They said if he followed Mira, he would catch her with her lover.

The prince followed her from the palace to a small temple. He heard her voice: "When can we be together, why do you leave me alone to weep without your sweet face, I can think of nothing but you."

Drawing his sword, the prince entered the temple. There sat Mira holding her beloved statue of Krishna, feathers from his crown strewn wildly about her. The prince laughed and took her home, she clutching her idol, the prince clutching her hand. He told his sister, "My wife is pure. She is mad, but pure."

Then the prince died. Mira mourned him, and turned with more fervor to Krishna. Her mother- and sister-in-law could not bear the insult. Who was this girl who refused to burn herself on her husband's funeral pyre, who neglected their goddess, who sang and fawned over the foolish, blue Krishna?

They called on the brother to poison Mira. But he was afraid of her, so he sent a servant to her room with a glass of mango juice. The juice was so filled with poison, the smell of it killed the cook who made it. Mira held the glass to her lips and drank. In her mouth, the poison turned to nectar.

The next day, when Mira went to the temple, her brother-

in-law replaced her mattress with a board of poison-tipped nails. When Mira returned from worship, she lay down to think of her Lord. The smell of roses filled the room. The nails had turned to petals and Mira slept, dreaming of her Lord.

Finally, the brother, sister, and mother expelled Mira from the household. They told her she must kill herself or be disgraced. She ran to the river, cradling the statue of Krishna in her arms, and jumped in.

She awoke on dry land, warm, living, blue arms around her waist, blue lips in her hair, the smell of roses, and her Lord, her Lord. He picked her up and set her on her feet, and Mira danced across the land singing of her Lord and their Love.

She died, an old woman. Krishna himself entered her room, playing his flute. He picked up the lifeless Mira and carried her away in his blue arms.

Again, I am dying. In a hospital bed in Arizona. I remember the shadow of my wimple, so much like a black wing. I remember sitting down, folding my hands in my lap. I closed my eyes; I waited.

There is the voice of Roderigo, my brother, come from Mexico to see me. I hear a woman say, "Take her things: a robe, a pair of black shoes, a rosary, a wimple, a page with ripped corners, torn from a book about a man named Heathcliff."

Blue, Without Sorrow

Roderigo says, "I remember her and Mama reading that. They hid it from Daddy (he did not approve of romances). She is younger than all of us boys, but always, she controlled us, especially after Mama died when Teresa was eight and I, eleven. You know, she did this to most of her books, tore bits from the pages she liked, and swallowed them. To be closer to the words, she said."

I am dying, and am not afraid, but impatient. The woman says, "Only thirty-one, such a tragedy." Roderigo says, "Again, she has done it again; it is what she wants."

How well he knows me.

Through the hospital blind a shroud of blue desert night crunches and cracks over my head. Hands, like fish, swim up my body. Patience, patience, Roderigo. I cannot wait any longer.

Acknowledgments

My deepest gratitude to Robin Lippincott and Sena Jeter Naslund.

Thanks to Sarabande: Sarah Gorham, Kirby Gann, Nickole Brown, Kristina McGrath, Charles Casey Martin, and Betsey Reed.

Thanks to Barry Goldensohn, Sarah Goodwin, Terry Diggory, Leslie Daniels, Sabrina Shakley, Kapil Gupta, Tara Maria, Katie Bradford, Ranjana Varghese, Jason Brown, Christopher Noël, Carol Anshaw, John Caughey, Roxanne Gupta, John Sloan, Lorrie Goldensohn, Greg McHale, Liza Tavtigian, Ann and Jim and clan Gordon (and Alan), Hugh and Janet Graham, Hugh Patterson Graham.

Thanks to Elwood S. Kent, Sr., Gagi Jhangiani, Chatru Jhangiani, Sita Vaswani, Julia Kent, and Nanikram Vaswani.

To Holter Graham, my heart, first and last reader. And to Lugnut.

And finally, to my parents, who taught me to live, love, work, and told me stories.

.

273

Some of the stories in this collection originally appeared in the following publications:

American Literary Review: "Bolero"
bananafish: "Bing-Chen" (formerly "Ming")
Catamaran: South Asian American Writing: "Five Objects in Queens"
Epoch: "The Pelvis Series"
Global City Review: "Possession at the Tomb of Sayyed Pir Hazrat Baba Bahadur Saheed Rah Aleh"
Hunger Mountain: "Twang (Release)"
The Louisville Review: "Blue, Without Sorrow"
Night Rally: "An Outline of No Direction"
Prairie Schooner: "Where the Long Grass Bends"
Shenandoah: "Sita and Ms. Durber"

Thanks to the above journals for their support. Thanks to Invisible Cities Press and Roger Weingarten for awarding the Italo Calvino Prize to "The Excrement Man."

The Author

Holter Graham

Neela Vaswani

lives in New York. Her short stories have appeared in numerous journals, including *Prairie Schooner, American Literary Review,* and *Shenandoah.* In 1999, she was awarded the Italo Calvino Prize. She is a Ph.D. candidate at the University of Maryland, and teaches in the brief-residency Master of Fine Arts in Writing program at Spalding University.